the ROAD to NOWHERE leads EVERYWHERE

TALES from the LANDS OF Arlington Green

BOOK ONE

Stephen B. Allen

DORRANCE PUBLISHING CO
EST. 1920
PITTSBURGH, PENNSYLVANIA 15238

The contents of this work, including, but not limited to, the accuracy of events, people, and places depicted; opinions expressed; permission to use previously published materials included; and any advice given or actions advocated are solely the responsibility of the author, who assumes all liability for said work and indemnifies the publisher against any claims stemming from publication of the work.

All Rights Reserved
Copyright © 2020 by Stephen B. Allen

No part of this book may be reproduced or transmitted, downloaded, distributed, reverse engineered, or stored in or introduced into any information storage and retrieval system, in any form or by any means, including photocopying and recording, whether electronic or mechanical, now known or hereinafter invented without permission in writing from the publisher.

Dorrance Publishing Co
585 Alpha Drive
Suite 103
Pittsburgh, PA 15238
Visit our website at *www.dorrancebookstore.com*

ISBN: 978-1-6461-0592-2
eISBN: 978-1-6461-0011-8

the ROAD to NOWHERE ~ leads ~ EVERYWHERE

TALES from the LANDS OF
✥ Arlington Green ✥

BOOK ONE

Stephen B. Allen

Table of Contents

Preface	5
Introduction	11
Foolish Notions	17
Fate	31
Village of the Fools	39
Village of the Damned	53
Holiday Outt	65
On the Road Again	79
Ales Well That Ends Well	87
All Manor of Foolishness	97
A Higher Hire	115
Reaching at Teaching	129
Pawn Takes Queen	137
Lessons Learned from a Desk	147
A Festival Occasion	165
Beautiful Voices…Beautiful Singers	185
Excerpt from "Dylan's Dilemmas"	209

Preface

When I first began to put words down on paper about a place called Arlington Green, the year was 2007. Forced to leave working for a living behind at that time due to failing health, I needed to find a purpose which would allow myself to still be able to look in the mirror at the person whom I had become and not see a worthless individual incapable of contributing something of value.

Ever since I was young, I always had a penchant for writing. Whether it was producing a process paper for a college-level Creative Writing class on the sport of Hunting Bees or creating foolish little short stories in order to lift the spirits of some special people in my life who needed a smile when they were down, putting words down on paper was something which I found I enjoyed. I won't claim that I did it well or had an extraordinary talent of any sort, but it seemed that I did have a knack for producing with the written word and I had fun doing it. In spite of having been terrible at diagramming sentences in English Class (to this day the term "dangling participle" still makes me think of Biology), apparently I could use all of the individual parts involved to write sentences which were ~~intelligent…enjoyable…clever~~…readable.

For more years than I care to recall (and there are some days when I find I cannot recall them at all), my efforts consisted of dabbling in re-writes of "The Night Before Christmas" for co-workers utilizing their names and our experiences. I was able to keep the pilot-light of my imagination lit through such simple little efforts, or by making up bedtime stories for my small children involving flying turtles as well as other flights of fancy. I discovered a very inescapable fact at that time—my stories were capable of quickly putting anyone to sleep.

Through the wonders of watching my children grow, as well as being introduced to the magic of grandchildren, I discovered how each one was their own special person capable of talents and abilities unique unto themselves. On the flipside however, I also saw how subjects which were easily conquered by one could be difficult for another. This in no way made one inferior or superior when compared to their sibling, it simply made them who they are. One child may be a wiz at math and nearly flunk Biology, while their brother may be just okay at understanding the complex processes of Algebra or Geometry, but at least he knows his a— from his elbow! Our brains all work differently, creating a unique individual unlike any other. If any further clarification of this concept is required, I offer this as proof; William Shakespeare was a writer…I am a writer…and if you read any of my work you can easily tell I am no William Shakespeare.

But then again, despite being acknowledged as one of the most celebrated authors in history, Mister Shakespeare never was capable of writing stories about Arlington Green, was he?

Still, I hate to see any child struggle and be held back from becoming a successful, confident young adult capable of reaching a potential beyond their wildest dreams. It was for just this reason that I wrote a children's picture book titled "The Alphabet Mall" back in 2006, where each shop has items for sale based upon a specific letter. This book's purpose was to help kids better understand their letters, and aid in their reading and writing.

Then came 2007!

Desperately needing something worthwhile to utilize my time, I decided that as "The Alphabet Mall" was a resounding success (I sold 14 whole copies), I would try my hand at creating another book for children focusing upon simple math concepts.

I decided to change the format by writing a short work where every chapter was a story involving different mathematical principles. Chapter One focused upon addition, Chapter Two was subtraction, with new subjects covered all the way up to Chapter Ten. I wanted to make the book fun as well as educational. Eventually, I came up with the idea of having the stories revolve around characters from the olden days of The Middle Ages, with a specific individual for every number from one to ten. Chapter One would highlight addition involving such people as a Knight (Sir Sixto), a Teller-of-Tales (Tenn), a Duke's son (Tre), etc. For the title of this project, I came up with "Tales from the Castle of Numbers."

But then a funny thing happened.

Putting together the framework for the book, I had the mathematical concepts for every chapter coupled with short cute stories to help make them understandable for children, and I began to write.

It was at this point where I began to run into difficulty.

My problem centered around…of all things…the characters! The further I got into the work, the more the characters continued to grow and develop until I realized they could not be contained within the confines of a basic children's picture book. Born within my imagination were not simple one-dimensional cardboard figures, but rather complex characters who—despite my best efforts, burst from out of the parameters I had placed upon them almost as if they were living breathing people with the need to grow further. As strange as it may sound, there were times when I did not think that I was writing about them. Instead, they were dictating stories of their lives for me to chronicle.

It wasn't long before I retired the idea of "Tales from the Castle of Numbers", and "Tales from the Lands of Arlington Green" was born. Names changed—Tenn became Dylan while Sir Sixto was now Sir Preston. Chapters became longer, consisting of storylines geared to an audience of anyone desiring to read an enjoyable, light-hearted book. I began the lofty ambition of creating a world of fascinating people and situations, hoping beyond hope that I could produce a worthy effort. My target, if I was capable of sustaining a project of this magnitude, was to write a work of perhaps fifteen chapters consisting of maybe 40,000-45,000 words. I had no idea if I was able to create a book so elaborate or lengthy as what I had envisioned, yet I knew that I had to try.

And then they went and did it again!

Those darn characters just would not stop. For every chapter I was able to complete, the ideas and storylines for three more would come to mind. By the time I was working on Chapter Six, I would come to the conclusion how in reality it was about to become Chapter Nine, as the new concepts I had come up with just had to fit between the present-day Chapters Four and Five. This lead to endless re-writes. By the time I had finally completed Chapter Ten, I would need to go back and re-do the first six due to the individuals in Chapter Eleven having outgrown the perceptions of the characters in the earlier work. To make a long story short, it was sometime in 2010 when I was looking as the Thirty-Six Chapter, 150,000-word monster I had created!

In an effort to shorten the work into something more manageable for an initial book, re-write number one hundred and sixty (?) involved trying to decide which chapters I would jettison, or those I would condense into smaller, less-wordy ones. The result of all this was I eliminated one chapter which lead to adding two more. What I had envisioned as one book became "The Road to Nowhere Leads Everywhere", "Dylan's Dilemmas", plus "Death Comes Calling". I had created THREE books, which constituted the initial trilogy of the epic series "Tales from the Lands of Arlington Green."

Finally, after all of the long hours, the late-nights, and the seemingly endless re-writes, I was done! I had created a work which I was very proud of and could go work on another project if I wished…after I took some time off to rest my overly-taxed and tired brain, of course.

Can you believe that they up and did it to me again?

I may have thought I was done, but then what did I know?

I'm just the guy who writes the stories.

Those very same characters whom I had created years ago decided that they were not ready to be retired. As far as they were concerned, they still had lots more living to do and wanted to do it with even more folks added to the mix. New ideas flowed into my head—which is not difficult to do as it generally is empty, but this time I put my foot down and told them NO MORE…

I WAS DONE!

A year or so later I put the finishing touches on "To the Victor Goes the Toils", the *fourth* book of the series.

Realizing at this point how I had absolutely no choice, I capitulated. "Treasure of the Crimson Corsairs" came to life, followed by "The Further Adventures of the Earl of Barnstable" as well as "Rascals and Royalty."

At *last* I was finished. The characters had become as real as I could make them, and the storyline was complete. With great personal satisfaction—coupled with more than a little sadness, it was time to bid a fond farewell to Arlington Green, to Barnstable, as well as to the people who had shared their lives within the confines of the series of books begun some 11 years ago.

PS. As I write this, book number eight titled "A King…The Pawn…and Two Queens" is already a work in progress, and I have this idea for an effort titled "Sins of the Fathers."

I never could win an argument.

Introduction

When I was younger and *supposed* to be growing up—I did indeed get older but the growing up part didn't end up sticking too well, I was always fascinated by stories of Knights and the legends of the Middle Ages. As our information sources in those days consisted of whatever books we checked out of the library, or the occasional black and white movie which would somehow find its way onto one of the three channels our TV would receive when the wind blew the antennae in the proper direction, the images I had of the people who lived during those times were always steadfast and serious. I saw one-dimensional caricatures of the person as drawn upon the page in the book. Kings were always regal, Queens never had so much as a hair out of place while dressed in the most opulent of gowns, and the Knights always appeared as if a dragon was right outside the door and they would be needed yet again to save the day.

It was once I began to realize that, regardless of station, these were indeed people capable of all things which everyday folks do such as laugh, cry, or even belch that I took to wondering what life was really like for those who lived during those times. Having no other point of reference to utilize beyond what I read in the history books about their deeds or dominant characteristics, in order to gain a perspective into the folks behind the facades, I projected what people are like in modern days into the figures who lived hundreds of years ago.

Realistic?

Not really, for the hard times they lived in demanded a tough lifestyle in order to survive. After all, sailors were still sailing off of that old flat world in those days. Perhaps those people who lived back then could not afford to be as compassionate as us sophisticates like to believe we have become in modern times. The individual of today has the benefit of additional hundreds of years of information and experience to form our ideals. The folks of The Middle Ages had much less to influence themselves, unless one could rely on tradition and often the status quo. The unexplained was everywhere—infantile science fighting to take its first baby steps while struggling against a world fraught with superstition and intolerance. While some may attempt to explain how it is that an apple falls from the tree to the ground, others knew without question that it was the sprites and pixies of the forest who caused it to fall—while the truly dangerous forbid any curiosity at all. The world of this age was seeking answers to questions it did not even know how to ask.

Feudalism was the mechanism by which the country was run. Individual Dukes, Barons, or Earls ruled their lands as they saw fit as long as The King got his taxes on time. Too often it was the iron fist under which they kept their people in line. Knights and men-at-arms fanned out throughout the countryside to impose the laws of the land as well as the whims of the Nobles. Life was harsh, and generally did not last very long.

There is a place which dwells within the realm of my imagination very similar to England of these later Middle Ages. Here, characters such as your typical self-centered Nobles, iron-headed Knights eager for the spilling of blood, or ignorant peasants still exist as one would expect of those times. Yet, within the confines of enclaves spread throughout the land, the winds of change are blowing. One such place is Arlington Green, where the hammer of despair does not fall quite so hard.

The people who reside there are not cut-out figures of time-worn characterizations pictured in the history books. Rather, these folks have real heart and soul...and brains. They have the capability for sympathy, empathy, and especially the ability to fill their lives with laughter, love, and song. Yet, when needed, they find within themselves the courage and strength of will to fight and die when those who are weaker pray for heroes.

For the moment, peace exists with their traditional enemies across The Channel who wear the coats of blue. However, it's fragile grip is slipping every day as men of power and greed see opportunities to be won through the blood of others.

Into this maelstrom of confusion and danger enters a young traveling Teller-of-Tales named Dylan. The harsh lessons which life had taught him at a younger age infuses within him a desire to find humor in everything he attempts. The concept of confusion is no stranger to this talented fellow, as his unlimited potential is kept in check only by his own propensity for uncertainty. His dream of traveling from town to town sharing with others stories formed within his imagination burns within his soul with a fire which cannot be quenched. Born with a talent for creativity, matched only by his stubborn nature and need to win any battle of wits he encounters, our young friend is about to leave the comfort of his familiar world behind and step out into the unknown.

Who is this young fellow, you may ask? An interesting question—one that he, himself, could not answer. At this point in his life, he is a young man of many jumbled pieces; he has seen twenty some-odd summers come and go, and yet has never sat under a full harvest moon with a young girl in his arms. He hides behind self-created walls to protect himself from emotional harm, yet unknowingly displays so much of his true self through the characters he creates. Expecting perfection from himself, as that is how he expects to be judged, errors and mistakes follow wherever he goes. For an intelligent young man, he has made the classic blunder formulated by the young from any walk of life. Mistakes will be made—that is how knowledge and wisdom grow from within.

Fail to make them, and you learn nothing.

Be *afraid* to make them, and yours is a life lost.

From the very beginning, the reader is captured by his boyish charm and mischievous deeds inspired by his refusal to grow up and accept the responsibilities of life which became thrust upon any other man in his early twenties. Narrated by young Dylan himself —he is a Teller-of-Tales after all, "The Road to Nowhere Goes Everywhere" follows his exploits from the first day he begins his journey traveling throughout the country attempting to ply his new-found craft. Confident in the knowledge that he had planned for any and all situations which could *possibly* be encountered along the way, it takes all of one day for him to come to the realization that he has absolutely no idea of what he is doing or even where he is going!

It is a credit to his tenacity (some might call it stubbornness) when he refuses to return to the comfortable life he had known in the city. Dylan is determined to blunder his way through what to him is the totally alien landscape of life in the Medieval countryside in order to follow his dream. The many mistakes he makes reveal a confused young man in turmoil, whose lack of self-confidence can only be overcome by his kind heart and quick mind. In spite of himself, Dylan begins to realize that it is acceptable to fail; the experiences gained by those many mistakes create a new person who is finally ready to grow. His indestructible sense of humor coupled with displays of intelligence and cleverness in dealing with his many challenges along the road are impressive, revealing the true potential of this young fellow.

Not all journeys involve the movement of one's feet, which Dylan comes to discover when after several years of traveling from village to village he happens upon a place where fate has guided his footsteps…the Village of Arlington Green. Deciding he has had enough of life upon the road, Dylan takes on a position as Tutor to the two young sons of The Duke and Duchess of Arlington Green and comes to live within their Manor as a member of the Staff. Continually frustrating The Duke—but most especially The Duchess—by his continued bouts of immaturity as well as refusal to lose at any challenge which comes his way, Dylan's true inner nature slowly begins to emerge as he stumbles from one encounter with disaster to another. Does Dylan, this immensely simple yet incredibly complicated, intelligent, foolish young man discover within himself the courage to put trust not only in himself, but more importantly place that trust in another? Can he allow his intense attraction for a young songstress he encounters named Robyn to overcome his inability to open himself up emotionally to the possibility of any lasting relationship with the young lady?

You need not fret for our young friend, for as you will discover through his own words, the path he is about to travel will create opportunities to confound everyone he meets. Yet once those pieces finally come together from his many experiences, the man he can become will be capable of deeds both great and yet terrible to behold.

If you wish to enjoy stories about Medieval Days containing people whom you will grow to laugh with—as well as at—or perhaps shed a tear for, welcome to the Lands of Arlington Green.

It really is well worth the trip.

Foolish Notions

How is the measure of a man weighed when he realizes how the life which he has chosen—or has, against his awareness, been chosen *for* him—is a mistake? If it is a sham which he is living, does he rail against the unfairness of his situation? Or does he simply shrug his shoulders marking his acceptance to the fates and pile up disappointing day after disappointing day until his life is mercifully ended? Perhaps he runs off on some romantic fantasy, questing for life's deep vast secrets only to slink home at some later day with the knowledge that he has been beaten down by the very notions which he believed to be truths *so* profound as to be capable of saving his immortal soul. Does he drown his sorrows in cups of ale too numerous to count? Or do the arms of a beautiful woman become his refuge, only to realize later in life how the sanctuary of these worldly delights do little to sate the thirst which drives him to sleepless nights haunted by the ghosts of who he *knows* he could have been?

Or maybe—just maybe—he puts down his quill and ink, stops writing romantic notions of what he believes to be profound observations never before realized by the common man, and leaves to go find his destiny!

While that may sound easy to do, for a young man barely in his twenties, life in this dangerous world in which we live is not conducive to grand bouts of artistic expression. Unless, of course, one is either very wealthy or very talented. Unfortunately, at this point in my life I was neither. It is too

THE ROAD TO NOWHERE LEADS EVERYWHERE

difficult to make it through every-day life with only romantic illusions of grandeur as your guide...unless one is *completely* delusional in which case welcome to my world!

Standing next to the sputtering torch hanging in the metal stanchion in the dimly-lit darkness outside of the front door of where I have comfortably called home these past nine years, with my few pitiful belongings including that ink and quill slung over my shoulders, I am grateful to the cacophony of noises emanating from the many taverns and dens of ill repute which constitute Perilous Alley. They mask the sound of the knocking of my knees due to mortal fear of the unknown! With one last longing glance at the door and the promise of the safety it contains, I gather my courage and turn my back upon the world which I have known. As I quietly trudge off into the nightly gloom to the accompaniment of the usual barking dogs in search of that destiny, I have no doubt that someday I will return to "The Alley." But when that day does arrive, I shall do so on my own terms.

Through the early-morning mist weaving its way through the dank recesses of the back streets I know so well, I saunter along as if without a care in the world. For that is how one successfully traverses the dangers of The Alley with his throat intact: act as if you belong there under the protection of some very powerful friends and it just may be believed. Hear everything—see what should remain hidden from your sight, and *never* let your hand stray from the reassuring touch of cold steel against the palm of your hand! These are the lessons which the smart survivors learn while the fools who forget them are usually found face-down in the gutters the next day by the members of The Night's Watch.

I will miss my good friend and benefactor "The Artist", the greatest forger in the kingdom and the man who found a newly-orphaned ten-year-old boy wandering aimlessly along The Alley in abject fear these eleven odd years ago. Had it not been for his intercession, I doubt that I would have lasted through the night as I was so far out of my element. He took me in; and with incredible patience, took a sullen, stubborn young ass with an attitude of how life was unfair and molded me into an apprentice worthy of his greatness. He gave me back my appreciation for life and all its wonders, while I gave him the best that my talents could provide.

And my love…I believe he *always* knew that.

Yet no matter how much I studied his craft and honed my abilities to replicate all manner of documents, at the end of the day I always found my quill scratching dabs of ink across blank parchment as characters and stories flowed from my mind, down my arm, and onto that parchment as effortlessly as if I were simply an observer to the experience. In time, I overcame my penchant for shyness as I began to paint my stories with the spoken word to any audience I could find rather than writing them down on manuscripts to be recalled sometime in the near future. In the smoke-filled taverns of Perilous Alley, I honed my craft, heaping mistake upon mistake until I found that I could actually capture audiences with my stories and carry them to places they would never be capable of visiting without my words as their guide. I took to wearing a floppy old brown hat the original shape of which had long been forgotten; were I to be seen traversing the alley or staking out a corner of the Capital's Central Square with that old formless hat upon my head, the initiated would know that a tale was about to be shared. The smart ones ran as fast as they could in the opposite direction, while those who had remained children at heart despite all that reality had managed to throw at them during their lifetimes gathered around me, their eyes dancing in the firelight as their focus turned inward in a quest to envision the magical world which I painted for them with my words. From other traveling Tellers-of-Tales, I learned how nuances in my vocal tone could flesh out characters and experiences better than entire paragraphs of written word. I could change stories amid sentence to better entertain particular audiences. Love becomes war, serious morphs into comedy extraordinaire...and unbelievably my empty pockets became depositories of coins in numbers beyond my wildest dreams!

Having seen or created enough fakes in his time, The Artist could recognize real talent when he saw it. Deep down, I believe he knew that he had lost me the first time he listened to one of my tales. My path was determined. However, the day when I was to take my first steps had yet to be decided.

With more than a little sadness on both of our parts, it was agreed that I would continue to work for him two more months...after which I would be free to go and find my destiny with his blessing. I threw myself into my work as I wanted to accomplish as much as I could as a way of showing appreciation to the man who had saved my life and mended my spirit. Long into the night to the sputtering of candle flames I would copy the script of some unknown scribe either omitting certain words or adding others until new ideas were born from old concepts for the benefit of whomever had employed our organization. We lived well, never went hungry, and wanted for little. Yet, while the attraction of living a secret life may be romanticized by some, the idea of simply re-creating the work of others kept me from settling into what could turn into a lucrative opportunity. It wasn't so much a question of right or wrong which I found perplexing, for our work took from rich men often corrupted and gave to other rich men hoping to attain that same level of corruption. My conundrum was more in that I would ponder other works written by these same scribes and wonder how *my* imagination and my ability would compare. I grew tired of adapting their words to fit the plans of others; I found I needed the challenge of utilizing my own words to create works which would hopefully be pondered and cherished by newer generations.

That and making enough money to live on was important of course... can't forget that one.

For days on end I thought and imagined what I would do if I were free to pursue my dreams until desire overcame fear and I started to make actual plans. Over and over in my mind I would figure out where I would go and how I would present myself until any and all possibilities were foreseen, any potential difficulties overcome. Routes of travel were carefully planned down to the tiniest of details encompassing time of year, weather to contend with, as well as villages with known resources to visit. The lessons of maximum preparedness for any and all unexpected situations which had been drilled into me by The Artist all these years had been well learned. I was ready and eager to begin the adventure of my life.

In time, the big day finally arrived when I made what had previously lived only within the confines of my imagination the foundation of all my future endeavors. I bid farewell to my teacher and friend, turned my back upon the life I knew, and was off to make the world mine with absolutely *nothing* to stop me.

Nothing except…reality!

And that is how later that same day I found myself standing at the southern edge of the city known as The Capital as the sun began to set in the west with absolutely NO idea of where to go or what to do next.

Eventually, I just began walking. I had no idea of where I wanted to go, nor had any idea in which direction my steps were taking me. What I *did* know however was how each one I took brought me closer to my goal and further from the life which I knew. Having lived all of that life within the confines of The Capital, walking out in the countryside in the dark was a whole new experience full of frightening sounds. I really did not know what to expect, so I expected *nothing* while trying to learn everything. Within the first several weeks, I learned quite a bit!

For instance, I learned that I should have walked more before I left The Capital, as by the end of the day, my feet and legs were awash in a sea of pain not easily diminished. I found that not eating was the norm as more often than not I was either on long empty stretches of road between towns or had long stretches of empty pockets when I finally arrived where food was to be found. I discovered how farmhouses with dogs kept wandering Tellers-of-Tales from finding shelter within barns as the pouring rains soaked everything which I owned...which became less and less the more villages that I visited as I was forced to sell off anything of value in order to get *something* to eat. I would occasionally be able to rustle up a small audience and come away with a coin or two. At first those instances were unfortunately few and far between. I had always expected to have to pay my dues as I learned the nuances of life on the road and honed my craft; what I had not counted on was how the don'ts would far outnumber the dues. As in—don't come strolling into a new town just as another wandering Teller-of-Tales has been run out after having been found in a barn with the Sheriff's daughter, or don't expect that marshlands have to end eventually just because the mosquitos are unbearable, and above all don't ever get some romantic boneheaded idea of how traveling for a living can be the life for you!

I learned how it gets really *dark* at night when there is no moon, and that if you continue to walk along the road during those hours when you cannot see anything, you will inevitably step in what the horses which you had spotted pulling a carriage ahead of you hours before had left behind. I discovered that during a lightning storm if your hair stands straight up it is not a good thing, and that if you are going to stop for the night you should get your fire started before daylight is completely gone or you cannot see what you are trying to do, as well as the very important lesson that shoes do not last nearly long enough.

I had always patted myself upon the back for having the smarts to begin my journey after the winter months had passed; I now had the knowledge that great whopping blizzards can and do pop up when they are no longer expected to! This also lead me to even greater questions in my quest for knowledge; whether it is better for the snow to stop falling and have it warm up or to take advantage of the unusual weather to pass through the marshlands without being bothered by incessant insects?

Oh, and just for future reference, no matter how cold a late season blizzard gets, the ice which it forms upon roadway ponds will never get sufficiently thick enough to support the weight of a Teller-of-Tales trying to take a shortcut across such a pond to find shelter in what appears to be an abandoned old barn. Speaking of which, did you know that swarms of bees will take up residence in the hollow walls of old structures allowing their populations to grow to astronomical numbers where they live in peace and quiet...until some moron trying to get out of a thunderstorm forces open the warped door of such a structure causing it to crash open against those same walls making them very angry?

I didn't.

I do now!

It has been said how the road can be a very demanding teacher, and I know this to be true; but not all that it teaches is bad or even dangerous. I met a woman healer in a small village which I had just been passing through without plans on staying. She was willing to teach me what roots and plants I could find in the fields along the roadway which were good to eat—and which were *not*. In exchange, I would tell a few stories to those villagers whom she knew were not long for this world as a way of taking their minds off of the inevitable. When we were out in the fields looking for plants, I half-jokingly asked if she knew how to brew a love potion. She gave me a strange look and said that I was my own love potion; I was just not ready to be properly mixed yet. I was told how all of the ingredients which made me whom I was would come together when I met the right girl, and then I would be irresistible. When I asked her how I would know if a girl was the right one, she just smiled and said that I would know.

Taking me around to several of the homes of the villagers she had been treating, I shared a tale or two with some older folks who were on their deathbeds and those family members caring for them. I don't believe that I will ever have a more appreciative audience; I know I shall never forget the smiles they shared. It was at the last house I was being taken to that first day where I met Martha Baker, a little six-year old girl who hurt so badly she could no longer even get out of her bed. She would just stare out of the window for hours at a time as she silently cried when the potion she was being given for her pain could control her agony—or lay screaming when it would not. Inspired by her need, I created some of my best stories about mysterious far-off lands and the adventures of the various people who lived there. I wove a tale or two with her that first day; she told me how if she closed her eyes as I spoke, she could almost imagine how she was there living out the stories in a magical land where the pain would not follow. Returning the next day, I shared with her a story about some little mice living in a great big castle. For the next several days I would make sure to visit her and whisk her away from the pain ravaging her frail little body to the world she saw in her mind where only happiness was allowed. I was treated to some of the last smiles this little girl would ever know.

I had planned on an over-night stay in that village—I left a week later after Martha had passed.

I had heard a few months afterwards how in a different town, my healer friend had treated a woman accused by another jealous villager of being a witch...and was burned at the stake for her efforts!

The road can be a *very* tough teacher, indeed.

I learned this lesson the hard way when a fellow Teller-of-Tales whom I had encountered on several occasions suggested that I should make my way to the village of Wilkerston as the people there were very open to paying well for a good tale. I was prepared to depart for his suggested town in the morning, until I had a conversation with the local Sherriff who had overheard the suggestion of Wilkerston and informed me that should I follow this 'friendly' advice, I would probably run afoul of highwaymen known to inhabit the woods outside of that town and quite possibly fail to survive the ordeal!

I really do hope that the poor unfortunate folk to whom I gave all of that Teller-of-Tales's clothes as well as his shoes—which I had 'acquired' by sneaking into his room in the dead of night, had put them to good use. I did not touch his purse, for that would have been outright stealing and that is something which I am not about. Can I help it if the Sherriff held the door to the room open for me to go inside and find garments to be donated to the destitute members of the local population?

Maybe next time that "gentleman" would think twice before attempting to send someone else to meet their fate in the hands of those who wield sharp objects around the throats of unsuspecting travelers without remorse!

And yes, I did sleep *very* well that night.

After six months of little more than carving out a career in starvation, I was fortunate to make the acquaintance of Mister Barnaby Higgins, a Quadruple W Teller-of-Tales who had been on the road for over 20 years. Having never heard of a Quadruple W Teller-of-Tales, I made the mistake of asking him for its meaning. With his usual carefree grin upon his rotund bewhiskered face, Mister Barnaby Higgins explained how this designation was of his own design, and that it stood for a Wonderful, Willing, Winsome, Wandering Teller-of-Tales. Apparently, I must have looked more like a Triple S—a Starving, Stumbling, Scarecrow—for Mister Higgins decided how I needed to be taken under *somebody's* wing and gain some practical knowledge before I became an emaciated *dead* Teller-of-Tales! Inviting me to travel along with him in order to teach me some tricks of the trade as we walked, I quickly agreed. I thought that I already knew how to tell a good and interesting tale and thus had little to learn on that subject. On the first day of our journey, I learned more from him in twelve hours than I had been able to teach myself in nearly two years!

The next three weeks would produce many of my favorite memories of my time spent traveling upon the road. By day, we would maintain either a good quick pace or a slow meandering one depending on the day of the week as well as how near we were to our destination. He taught me how all towns or villages were not the same; if you were headed to a large farming community, there was only one day each week in which to be able to gather a sufficient audience for your tale and that was Sunday.

"These people work the fields or tend to their flocks at least six days a week," he explained before I could even ask why. "The only day when they have any free time is right after they meet for Church. Couple that with the fact they have already gathered your audience for you if you are patient and wait for the service to be over. You arrive in such a town on a weekday and you will be facing crowds which you can count on the fingers of one hand," he said. "Thus we either hurry or take our time. If you treat every day the same instead of planning out your journey depending upon the nature of the surrounding territory, you will never have any significant money earned," he explained, the jowls of his chubby face (which matched his chubby body nicely) shaking as he laughed.

In this manner, I learned about seeking larger more prosperous towns for holidays and festivals as chances are folks would be available for several days' worth of decent audiences, and how to keep some of your money in your shoes or socks in the unhappy event you should be robbed. In short, all kinds of information which 20 years of experience had taught him, and I was being freely offered it all.

At night, by the shimmer of the flames of our fires, we swapped stories. He always waited until the next day to critique my efforts—said he didn't want to put a damper on my enthusiasm for the tale. After a short while, I began to offer my opinions of how I could have done better before he even got the opportunity to tell me how to improve. That made him very pleased, as he said to always consider in which ways you could improve your presentation or performance.

"Wake up every morning with the urge to be better than you were the day before," he instructed. "Even if you had not made a presentation that day." It was advice which I would always recall and keep close to my heart.

No matter how much we were enjoying each other's company, one morning he informed me how later that day when we came to the fork in the road, we would each go our separate ways. "Bird's gotta' learn to fly," was how he put it. It was a very sad moment when we arrived at that separation point. I will never forget him nor the many lessons he shared with me. Had he not given me the benefit of his wisdom, it is quite possible I may have had to give up my dream and never gotten to where I needed to be later on in life.

Work with me here. I was a city kid who had never been on my own since the age of ten. I knew the ins and outs of a place like Perilous Alley, but one does not exactly find many such alleys in the open fields and small villages or hamlets dotted alongside the dirt road providing the lifeblood of food and various goods which kept the beating heart of The Realm alive. (Darn that was good!). When I left The Artist that morning, I was so certain I knew it all; very soon I realized how I had not even learned the right questions to ask! But to my credit, I was not too proud to take advice, ask the questions which I could figure I needed to know the answers to, but above all—I *never* gave up! I may have sighed…I may have cried…I never lied…and I never died! (Now that was *really* good; I have to stop and write that one down before I forget it!).

This is what I do all day as I walk the many leagues from town to town…I think.

Yes, I do!

As I am already wandering, I let my mind do the same; I just hope to catch up to it by the end of the day. With some of the thoughts or questions

I come up with sometimes, I begin to wonder if maybe it has gotten so far away from me that I may never get it back.

Let me give you some examples of several of the more interesting notions I have come up with during my travels and you be the judge of whether I did indeed regain my mind or better yet if I should even try.

I have read stories how during wars back in ancient times, entire cities of stone would be burnt to the ground. Just how is it that one gets stone to burn? And if stone originally was ground to begin with, how far does it have to burn to get to where it was in the first place?

I hear there is a land across the water where there are no snakes—absolutely none! I wonder what would happen if I went there with a snake in my bag, and when no one was looking took it out, threw it on the ground, and exclaimed "Look what I found!"

How many cows died of starvation until one finally thought *'Hey that grass looks interesting.'*

A drop of rain falls from the sky and lands in a pond. This pond feeds a brook, which gains strength and becomes a stream. By and by the stream becomes a river, which eventually flows into the sea. That drop has done its job, right? What about the poor drop that lands on your head and dries there...is that one dead?

Why is it that people name their children after flowers (Rose, Lilly) or shrubbery (Holly, Fern) and yet you never hear of anyone named after a tree (Dogwood, Oak, Pine)? What do people have against trees?

Ever watch a chicken? Me neither. As far as animals go, they are so darn boring! Rather tasty if the truth be known, but still not worth watching.

If day always follows night, and seasons will always be when they are supposed to be, do you suppose that storms are a result of God getting bored?

Sometimes I think that particular words are purposely spelled wrong. An example? You have man, and you have woman. In my mind, their name should have been spelled woe-man as us guys certainly could have used the warning!

Why is it that birds think the seeds they carry in their poop will grow in my hat?

Have you ever stopped and watched an ant at work? They are amazing in the amount of non-stop work they do. I finally had to stop watching—I was too exhausted.

Horse eats grass—poops on grass—poop helps grass grow; a very nice closed system.

If you were given the opportunity of living one day again, which would it be? My choice personally would be the day after I died, thank you.

I think I know a secret; it's why God made seagulls and pigeons. We all know what they are famous for, right? So, every time they err in their calculations and do not hit you in the head with you-know-what, we look to the sky and say, 'Thank God it missed'. I think that He appreciates the attention.

Besides these crazy thoughts of mine, I do spend *some* time wisely and come up with ideas for new stories or clever lines to add to existing ones. On a good day I might be found under a tree upon the side of the road for hours, my ink and quill virtually flying over the piece of parchment in my hands as a tale unfolds. Other days I might be found under a tree upon the side of the road for hours…sleeping. To me, that is the allure of the life which I have chosen; I have no set schedules as I have no one to answer to but myself. What I choose is what I do.

Do I have *some* restraints upon absolute freedom of choice? Of course I do—most of them have to do with food and the acquisition of such. I am my own boss, the cook of the operation, the food procurement committee, the one in charge of making the night fire…in short, I fill many positions (actually all of them) within the Dylan Ainsley Organization. It is an unfortunate truth that while I have a complete idiot for a boss, the crew whom I have working under me is made up of total morons!

Fate

The blanket held over my head had long ceased to provide any protection from the pouring rain drenching everything in sight. Soaked beyond its capabilities to repel moisture to any degree, tiny waterfalls poured from my equally ineffective hat down my collar to form streams of water cascading further down my body. Joined together into several raging rivers, their journey ended as they became one with the ever-growing Lake Dylan which had formed in the seat of my pants!

Having been caught out in the open with no cover to protect myself from this sudden deluge, I placed all of my hopes upon the notion that the storm would pass quickly. Half an hour later, after having nothing to do but count the number of times my body shivered uncontrollably between bursts of lightning, I emptied the contents of Lake Dylan by rising to my feet. If I was going to be wet and miserable, I might as well try to gain some manner of advantage and continue on with my journey.

Accompanied by the sounds of my water-logged boots squishing in the mud, I set off at a decent pace—all things considered. In time, the incessant rain finally came to an end, blessed sunlight beginning the process of removing deeply-grooved wrinkles from the tips of my fingers. Alas, for my feet and toes there was no hope as the ridges there would remain until I could dry out my footwear over a most-welcomed fire.

It was when I was joined in my journey by an old familiar traveling companion known as "chafing" that I did my best to find some thoughts for my mind to focus upon. It did not take long for a subject I had often pondered to roost under my slowly-drying hat. What had influenced me to decide upon this outrageous life of traveling all over the country in the first place?

Try as I might, of all of the notions in this life which I have been unable to wrap my head around and arrive at a final conclusion is this question: Do I believe in fate, or do I not? I have pondered upon this riddle for as long as I can remember. Even as a small child, I wrestled with the terrible purpose which decisions can create within one's daily life. When I was confident that I had finally found the answer to this dilemma upon numerous occasions, some incident would suddenly occur to prompt a 180 degree turn in my logic. Certain beyond a shadow of a doubt how I had indeed finally solved this most curious conundrum once and for all by embracing the exact opposite of my thinking from the previous day, tomorrow would arrive. Before the setting of the sun, I came to realize that I had been wrong in my prior day's assumptions and was in reality no closer to definitively answering my own grand question than I had ever been before!

I imagine that my quest for the truth began in the tenth year of my life with the tragic death of both my parents. For what felt like endless days and especially nights, I found myself staring out into space from whatever shelter I had been able to locate that day in order to escape from the elements, all the while trying to discover some understanding how a series of events so bizarre could occur in such a precise sequence resulting in my becoming an orphan at so tender an age.

What if my Uncle Harold had been watching where he was going in the market on one spring day and never bumped into a young lady named Katherine—which resulted in Harold knocking all of the produce she was carrying in her basket onto the ground? Chances are, he never would have had the chance to converse with her as he helped gather her vegetables from the ground. No conversation, no opportunity to get to know each other, wouldn't you say? Therefore, the two of them falling in love and deciding to marry on the second weekend of September would never have occurred. No wedding, no need for my parents to rent a coach with which to travel for two days to arrive at the venue. Yet, even *if* somehow this wedding had been a foregone conclusion, had they not picked that particular weekend to celebrate their union, chances are I would have not been so ill and I could have attended the event, instead of having to stay home under the care of one of the neighbor ladies.

If I *had* been with them, would they have left to return home exactly when they did, or could I have delayed their departure even if only by a minute or two? Perhaps I would have felt the need to have them stop along the way for me to run into the bushes, throwing off their timetable even by the smallest of margins. If so, then the hornet which had just been flying by as the horse pulling their carriage arrived at the same place and time would not have become lodged in the horse's mane and begun to sting about in desperation! Thus, the horse would not have panicked and would not have attempted to escape the painful stings by running away uncontrollably and into the small ditch formed on the side of the road by a recent passing shower. Even *with* a wildly-running horse, if the rain had been any less intense, the probability was that no ditch would have formed at all.

As it was, both right wheels slammed into the ditch while the left ones remained stable upon the roadway. Having seen the inevitability of the crash, the driver of the carriage jumped free at the opportune moment. My parents, riding inside of the carriage, had no such visual warning. The subsequent violent impact and tumbling of the carriage over and over killed both of my parents instantly.

The driver survived. Had he not, I don't suppose I would ever have known the bizarre sequence of so *many* unconnected events played out in such a precise pattern resulting in the only people whom I had ever loved being taken from me for all time.

My Uncle Harold was the only remaining family I had left in the world. Being newly-married, my Aunt Katherine did not wish to be made responsible for a ten-year-old boy. Thus it was decided that I would be given over to the authorities for placement into one of the many Orphan's Asylums located throughout the Capital. Before I could be taken away to be put into what I had heard was nothing more than a sanctioned workhouse, I grabbed whatever clothes I could carry and ran away.

In one terrible moment, life had taken a happy ten-year old boy from the comfort of the life he had known and unceremoniously discarded him upon the street with the rest of the garbage. Without money or food, I had to try to somehow learn how to survive in a harsh new environment and fend for myself as I wandered aimlessly throughout The Capital. Hungry, dirty, and with no hope, I happened to chance upon a small alcove to get out of a driving rain in a place called Perilous Alley. If I hadn't sneezed just as I saw a pair of shoes passing my hiding spot, the Gentleman would never have stopped and bent down to look into the alcove to determine the source of the noise. Had he not, I never would have seen the first smile I had encountered in weeks, nor been offered a place to stay and something to eat by the Master Forger who lived in The Alley and had been out at that moment procuring supplies for his latest endeavor.

Thus my years with "The Artist" came to be.

So many events. So *many* opportunities for even one piece of the puzzle to fall out of place by just a moment or two and my life would have had momentous differences. Would those differences have been good or bad—who could say? Who knows, perhaps my family would have had a candle topple over in the middle of the night and we all would have ended up dying in the fire one week later. Or perhaps the result would have been the same and somehow I alone survived.

Was my path in life already laid out for me by some all-knowing deity, in some gigantic book written in an unknown language, long since forgotten by all except its author? I like to think not, for would not such a scenario indicate the absence of free-will and the ability to create your own destiny by the choices you make?

Unless, of course, the person you *were* determined what manner of choices you were to make. In which case, this pawn was back to square one on the chessboard of life with all of my future moves choreographed in advance for some purpose I was unable to fathom. It may be a flaw in my character, but there is something about being told what to do by predetermination, chance, or some destiny which does not sit well with me. Never has. I have become who I am by keeping true to the man I believe myself to be. Have I made mistakes? Countless number of them, in fact, and I strongly suspect I shall make many more. Yet in the course of my blunders, not only have I gained wisdom from their creation but I have relied upon myself and my mind to arrive at their results. There was not some voice in the back of my head telling me what I was supposed to do.

Even if there had been, I would not have listened—probably gone and done the opposite, if the truth be known.

I can't imagine *why* I have been called "*stubborn*" so often by The Artist...or anyone else I have generally come into contact with for that matter.

Looking back upon my life of the past decade, as I often have these past several years while endlessly walking alone, I have come to realize even more just what a debt of gratitude I owe to the man I had come to love nearly as deeply as my own father. While he may have been strict in manner, I now recognize that this aspect of his personality was a natural result of his need to be precise in his work. I just wish I had come to this realization sooner, then perhaps my tendency of being overly stubborn and refusing to lose any challenge could have been lessened to a degree where I may have remained within The Capital after all.

Was it fate that caused us to have a terrible argument one evening where I threatened to leave and in his temporary anger, The Artist said that I would never have the strength of will to pursue the life of a traveler? No matter how many times we both apologized to the other for what had been said that night, the seed had been planted and the challenge made.

Damn my stubbornness!

It is for exactly this reason why I could never go back until I have made something of myself. No matter how grateful I am to him for all that he has done for me, for all that he has taught and given to me, for all that I have become—I cannot return as a failure. In my heart, I am certain he would not care as to the nature of my return and would welcome me with open arms regardless of my stature. After all, who could possibly imagine that a forger of all people, used to living within a cocoon of precision would reach out his hand to a shivering helpless ten-year-old boy knowing quite well that his perfectly-planned existence would be shattered by the raising of a child—and an exceedingly stubborn one at that?

No, I have steeled my resolve; until I feel that I can return, I will not! Perhaps that is why the road has become the only home I will admit to.

I *will* see him again. I must—if for no other reason than to tell him in my own words everything he already knows.

Without meaning to brag about myself, I do believe that I have talent and skill with using words to create stories for many to enjoy. Did such talent *require* that I take to the road as a traveling Teller-of-Tales going from town to town? Could I not just have easily—more so if I am being honest—stayed within the confines of The Capital and plied my trade free of the ties to Perilous Alley? I would have kept drier on many days, better fed on most of them, and who knows, I may have become somewhat well-known and lived a most comfortable life.

Except that is not who I am. I, Dylan Ainsley, had decided for myself that the lure of living a life free of encumbrances and traveling throughout the Realm spoke of adventure, plus an opportunity to experience wonders which I never could have seen had I remained in The Capital, and…

Wait a minute!

Did I just say "*spoke*" of adventure? I can recall feeling the urge to follow that path for years before I gathered the courage to set out on my own. I remember listening to traveling Tellers-of-Tales one would encounter within the taverns of Perilous Alley almost as if I were in a trance and could virtually *see* their notable experiences through mine own eyes. As a moth is attracted to a flame, such would I be to the news that a new traveler was going to be sharing stories of his adventures upon the road.

I need to work this out for a moment.

When I say "spoke" of adventure, I recall hearing my own thoughts within my head. If one were to take this observation literally, it would mean that I could have been under the delusion that they were my own thoughts when in reality I was listening to a voice implanting ideas within my own mind! Now, as I recall, moths have no choice in how they respond to lights in the dark; it is predetermined by nature that they do this. Does a "voice" indicate what my future should be, while I have absolutely no choice in how I respond? It appears that I was about to walk upon a path laid out by someone or something for me to follow.

Sounds like a serious case of fate to me!

It appears once again that I have walked the path of indecision only to realize I have gone in a complete circle and have returned to my original starting point.

When I made the life on the road my own, I had way too much time on my hands as I walked from town to town. Naturally, my mind would focus endlessly upon these questions until I became obsessed by such notions where, should I come to a fork in the road, I could be found studying both tracts for hours while trying to decide which one I was *supposed* to take.

THE ROAD TO NOWHERE LEADS EVERYWHERE

Was it decreed that I should walk for another hour until it began to get dark, or should I instead stop for the night and get a nice warm fire going? What could be the possible results of either action? What could the terrible consequences be if I made the wrong choice? Before I went completely stark-raving mad, one evening as I contemplated the dancing flames of my campfire, I came to the realization of how such small insignificant matters could not *possibly* have an overpowering lasting effect upon my future. The next morning while armed with my new-found insight, there was a fresh spring in my step as with a lightened heart I stepped off towards whatever the road may have in store for me, until…later that afternoon when I stopped dead in my tracks by the notion that maybe last night's conclusion was just what I was *supposed* to have arrived at.

Fortunately, before I could go permanently out of my mind, a strange thing happened. Thanks to events and situations which I had encountered during my journey, I began to gain a confidence in my abilities and especially in myself. With this confidence came the realization that regardless of situation, I could rely upon myself and my judgment to make the right choices—or at least *most* of them.

Who knows? Perhaps this conundrum will be settled once and for all in the town I shall be arriving at in the morning.

I believe that the name of this town painted upon the sign I just passed was…Brackensburg.

Village of the Fools

Nearly two years can seem like forever when you are wandering along the road. You see many wonderful things and terrific people; these are the memories which you cherish around a solitary fire in the dead of night. You want memories such as these, for you have only your mind as a companion on an empty lonely road, and minds have a way of constantly bringing to your attention people and places where your experiences were not pleasant. The unpleasant memories are the ones you re-live over…and over…and over again. If you be awake, you attempt to force your mind to thoughts of elsewhere; should you be asleep, you wake up screaming from the visions of hell you can never escape!

Being a traveling Teller-of-Tales, it is inevitable how I am always asked the same question no matter where I go: "Were you there?" I am assured by all of the other Tellers-of-Tales whom I happen to meet upon the road that they receive the same inquiries from their audiences at the various villages through which they travel as well. It is at this point where my contemporaries break out into voracious grins and indicate how they always answer in the affirmative, for what better story to tell than one which the audience has already shown an intense interest in?

What's the difference between these other Tellers-of-Tales and myself? To begin with, I always respond by declaring how not only was I *not* there as I do not even know where 'there' *is* but that I have no idea of what they are referring to! And I certainly do not announce to an audience which I am in front of any differently as I don't need to make coin for my pockets *that* badly. The sad reality is I know all too well just what is being referred to and can identify all of the lies which are being circulated among the population; for unlike any of these pretenders, the damnable truth is that I *was* indeed there!

I was there—and the knowledge of the experience will haunt my dreams until the day I die!

The *where* to which they refer was a small river hamlet until recently known as Brackensburg; today any reference to that name has since been stricken from all written history, its evil name as black as the burnt out remains of what had been people's homes as well as their very lives. The *when* was within these few months gone past. As to the why? The answer to the *why* is that only God knows—unless you should happen to speak to the shades of those who called Brackensburg home until the night when an entire town was struck by a blinding madness that caused them to lose their grip not only on their sanity but their humanity as well. Perhaps the dead would be willing to share their tale, for I am not.

Even now, on the nights when I awaken shaking to the sound of my own screams as their faces haunt my dreams or I attempt to make some sense of their madness or understand how it overcame them, I begin to feel myself slipping deeper into a melancholy which is slowly eating away at my spirit. I know for a certainty that someday soon I shall be able to finally understand them as I will become one with them.

The last grown survivor will be claimed and the secret will die with me for all eternity. Or at least until a time when the confines of Hell become no more!

That is why I am putting this tale to parchment. Upon its completion I shall have it sent to The Artist in hopes that in some small measure I shall be freed if the truth be known so as to hopefully never be repeated.

I had arrived that cursed day at the Brackensburg Village Green within minutes of the Church services having ended. This was perfect for me as a crowd of folks had already been gathered in the right place to listen to my stories for the day. Hoping that The Padre had preached about generosity and charity as this might make for a very profitable stop, I studied the scene before me to decide where the largest group had congregated (no church pun intended) for that would be the best place to begin my stories.

While surveying the landscape, I happened to notice a rather rotund gentleman clothed in a plain brown robe approaching me. My assumptions that this was the village's Padre were soon verified when he introduced himself as Padre Bartholomew while he shook my hand in welcome. Guessing correctly as to the nature of my work, he next did a very strange thing. Pulling me closely so as to keep from being unheard, he whispered how it would be in my best interests to get away from this village…NOW!

I had anticipated having to explain to some Church authority how the tales which I had chosen would in no way diminish the piety of the people on this special day but rather impress upon them the beauty and splendor of the gifts which we as people had been granted by The Creator. Never had I anticipated receiving such a dread warning to leave immediately.

Hearing what had been my vision for the tales I would tell, he smiled with his mouth, but not his eyes. "Were that you had arrived several weeks ago with just your message," he lamented as he looked over the crowd standing on the green and not leaving. "Perhaps you could have prevented this! I did my best, but they would not listen to me at all."

Curiosity having gotten the best of me, I turned away from The Padre to observe the crowd once again, this time with jaded eyes as a means of seeing what Padre Bartholomew was referring to.

It was a strange sight which met my view; one which I had to observe, try to make sense of what I had witnessed, and re-observe to make certain how my eyes were not playing tricks on me.

Instead of people milling about in small groups or individually greeting their neighbors with smiles indicating warm feelings, I saw quite the opposite. There was no milling or mingling as the crowd had for some obscure reason separated themselves into two distinct sections with a short spacing between them as if this were a zone not to be crossed by anyone who did not want to take the consequences. Given the looks of anger upon their faces as they heaped taunts and curse words most-foul at the person or people opposite of them across the divide lent me to believe that those consequences could be very drastic and painful indeed.

Never had I seen such behavior from a group of people who in reality needed each other in order to survive. What had happened here to cause such strife and, dare I say, *hatred*!

Turning back around to address the Padre, I could see the sorrow in his face as he gazed down upon his people. "I tried," he whispered to himself as if I were not there. "I tried so *hard* to prevent this. I did everything I could think of to do and I have failed."

Grabbing his robe at the shoulders to break the spell he was under, I could see his eyes re-focus on me with the light of reason in them once again. "Padre, what in God's name has happened here?" I asked while trying to comprehend what I saw on the Village Green.

"God has nothing to do with this," he said sadly as we both backed off a space so as to be heard above the angry din. When we had retreated far enough, he began to attempt to explain that which I had witnessed.

"It all started rather slowly about two months ago," he began. "The harvest had come in, better than had been expected in fact, which meant there would be some extra money available to be utilized for the good of all the village. While one would think that such news would be met with rejoicing and good-will, it had just the opposite effect," he said slowly shaking his head back and forth.

"You see, ever since last year when monies were allocated so as to make one segment of the village happy, the others who wanted the bounty spent in an all-together different fashion had been stewing. At first, comments were made in the company of all which were totally unnecessary and frankly in bad taste. Names began to be thrown at each other. Soon factions were forming which began to separate the entire village as well as individuals within families themselves! Once they formed these factions, there was little common ground to be found to be shared between them; soon enough there was none."

"They've even taken up names for themselves," he told me. "On one hand we have a group who wants to see the village grow; they call themselves "Organization for Public Growth" or "OPG," as they say they stand for the public good. On the other side of the fence are the people who belong to "Objective Dissent," a faction who believe that they and they alone know what is best for the people of this village."

"So you are saying that the population of this village—the *entire* population has actually formed in separate established groups?" I asked in amazement while having difficulty in believing what I was hearing. "How does anything get done if nobody is willing to agree with each other?"

"That's just it…while people are still working for their own personal benefit, nothing is being accomplished for the good of the village!"

Still trying to wrap my head around this business, I asked him to give me examples of what he was referring to.

"There has been an increase in highwaymen attacking villages in this area in spite of the best efforts of the local Lord," he explained. "In order to protect the village as well as its inhabitants, the Organization for Public Growth suggested that a wall be constructed around the village to make it difficult to attack. Many would think this to be a sound idea; yet the Dissenters voted it down, saying that such an idea would discourage any new folks wanting to move here from feeling welcome as well as could discourage trade with our neighboring towns and villages. The OPG countered with the point that a wall would not only discourage bandits but provide real protection should the army who wears coats of blue decide to invade us again as had happened in the past. The Dissenters scoffed at the idea, saying the war happened years ago and that this was a new day. If we were to extend the olive branch to our traditional enemies and seek a real peace, then we would not have to have those concerns any longer was their argument."

I could not believe what I was hearing. "What does the local Lord say about all of this?" I asked, as usually it is they who have the final say in how things are to be run in the villages they "own."

"The Earl is an old man who frankly has grown tired of the constant bickering," the Padre explained. "He figured that he had an ingenious solution and decreed that an additional Village Elder would be added to The Council of Elders so as to allow for the breaking of any tied vote and end the stalemate three to two. An election was held and when the final votes were counted the Elder presented by the Organization for Public Growth won. Naturally this led to the charge by the Dissenters that the results were falsified and should be changed as *their* man had actually won.

"The election was held only last week; you can see for yourself what the marches held by both sides this day have resulted in," he announced sadly on the verge of tears.

That explained the Dissenters chanting of, "He's not *my* Elder!"

Taking a moment to look over the scene unfolding before us, I noticed for the first time that on either side of the line, what I concluded to be banners were flapping in the breeze. Padre Bartholomew explained to me that these were the symbols of both parties: the hare was the symbol of the Organization for Public Growth who favored swift and bold action, while naturally its exact opposite, the turtle, signaled an allegiance to the Objective Dissenters as it represented slow and measured actions.

It was obvious that something drastic needed to be done. Yet how could a town whose own people did not even trust their neighbor have the inclination to listen to each other? The scenario I saw before me did not lend itself to compromise in the least!

But what about the intrusion of an outsider? Had my 'old friend' fate lead me to this village at just this moment in time for a reason? Would someone other than a member of the village be seen as enough of a threat for them to come together even for a short time and deal with the rabble-rouser? Looking upon the face of Padre Bartholomew and seeing the depth of his anguish and pain, I figured who possible could be better at rousing rabble than I?

Seeing the look of hope upon the good Padre's face when I suggested that perhaps I could be of some help, I sauntered down into the midst of the sea of angry faces; yet try as I might, I could not get the attention of more than a handful of folks at a time. My pleas of "If you can't stop screaming at each other, how can you possibly talk through your problems to arrive at solutions?" fell upon deaf ears. Nobody was interested in talking, for talking holds the risk that one may find yourself agreeing with some of the opposition's points and lose some of their self-righteous indignation. Apparently, screaming down any different opinions freed them of being convinced they could be wrong and therefore made them feel powerful.

I asked the good Padre if he had a piece of cloth, something to draw with, plus a short length of rope. As he ran (which was a sight unto itself!) to the church to gather the items I had asked for, I formulated what I hoped to be a plan which would result in at least enough of the villagers recognizing the foolishness of this counterproductive activity and ultimately result in yours truly not getting his fool-self killed!

A deep gasping for breath indicated the return of the good Padre. Quickly preparing my materials, I asked him to wish me luck as I prepared to carry out my plan. He obviously decided rightfully that I needed more help than I had asked, for as he gave me a blessing to see me on my way.

It had to have been just my imagination, but I could have sworn I heard a prayer signifying the beginning of a funeral emanating from behind me in the direction of the good Padre as I strode down into the fray. I went to the very end of the line separating both factions who were now on the brink of open warfare just waiting for a spark to set them off.

Taking the length of rope, I proceeded to force my way through the still open pathway with a continual "pardon me" or "excuse me" helping create *some* open space all the while trailing the length of rope behind me on the ground. Every few feet I would lift my head first to one side and then the other offering a wide smile and asking how they were feeling today.

As if re-enacting the parting of the Red Sea, space between the factions was opening up as folks stopped screaming at one another and watched in disbelief as some crazy fool passed between with a piece of rope trailing behind. Wicked words literally died upon lips without being said as stunned silence was the only way to handle the sight before them. From his position far enough from the fray, I'm certain that Padre Bartholomew was able to track my progress by where bellowing ceased and fingers began to point.

Countless people asked me just what the hell was I doing, but I refused to answer. Instead I just continued with the smiling and inquiring about their health and such. Finally gaining the other end of the line, I straightened up, pantomimed the wiping of sweat from my brow, and with the admission of "Well that was quite tiring," turned about and began the process once more in the opposite direction. Arriving in what I surmised to be the center of the crowd, I finally stopped and stood for a moment while keenly aware how all eyes were upon me and my antics. From this vantage point, I knew that all gathered there would be able to hear me; what could not be determined unfortunately was for how long they would bother to listen.

Announcing how my rope was getting quite heavy, I asked if anybody would hold it for me awhile. Finally, I was able to convince a kind soul in the Dissenters to take it from my hands…which naturally resulted in a member of the OPG demanding to hold the opposite end!

Pausing to allow the sight of my rope being held by both parties, but before a tug-of-war to break out, I announced in my best Teller-of-Tales voice how I guess it was not true what I had heard—after which I remained silent to see if I was drawing them out. Finally, the Dissenter who had originally taken the rope asked me what wasn't true?

"Oh, nothing special," I announced while pausing once again to keep their attention. "I had heard that it would take a miracle for both of your sides to agree to do anything together. Must not be the case then, wouldn't you say?" I asked while pointing to the rope which naturally was immediately thrown to the ground by both handlers.

Simply shrugging my shoulders and saying, "Oh well," I proceeded to pick up one end of the rope and continued to drag it behind me once again.

"Mister, just what in the hell are you dragging that damn rope for?" a rather large and intimidating OPG thug demanded before I had taken half a dozen steps.

"Oh, you mean *this* rope?" I asked while holding it up for his inspection.

"Yeah, that there rope. Why do you keep pulling that stupid piece of rope?" he demanded.

"Well friend, have you ever tried to *push* one?" I asked with a shade of a smile. "Damned near impossible to do I must say."

I did hear a few scattered brief laughs escape from the horde once they understood what I had said. It did not last long, but at least they were there.

"Say, just who in the heck are you?" a Dissenter wondered loudly to a supporting chorus of both factions wondering as well.

"Well, my friend, my name is Dylan, and up to just a few minutes ago I was a Teller-of-Tales by trade," I told him. "But thanks to the inspiration of you good folks I have taken up a new calling." I unfurled the small banner which I had rapidly created from the materials given to me by Padre Bartholomew. "I have decided to create my own faction," I announced to all while holding the image of a rudimentary snake up for all to see. "I figured that only two factions were not enough for a hamlet the size of yours, so I am forming another for anyone who wishes to join."

My announcement was met by dead (bad choice of words) silence.

At least it was a peaceful silence…I felt pretty fortunate about that.

"Look here, we know that *we're* right. Just what makes you think that we would want to split onto a different faction?" a Dissenter growled only to have an OPG member repeat his statement virtually word for word, once again proving that both sides could find something to agree upon—until they realized that they *had* just agreed upon something and ceased to make a sound.

Taking the biggest chance which I had risked to this point, I plowed forward while hoping that the good word Padre Bartholomew had put in for me with his Boss had been heard and was working for me.

"Friend, what you don't yet realize is that each and every one of you already *has* split away from the norm and probably doesn't even *know* it!" I answered and immediately shut up to wait for the inevitable.

A growing chorus of "What the hell are you talking about?" coupled with "I'd never ever be anything but an 'OPG/Dissenter' member," mixed with a large number of "This guy is crazy," comments flooded the crowd. If I had not taken that moment to tear my faction's stanchion to pieces, who knows what may have happened.

Having the effect I desired by quieting the crowd once again, when I was asked the inevitable question of why I did that, I replied that I no longer needed it as it had outgrown itself and was in reality at the moment *three* separate entities. Now *both* sides demanded an explanation until they each realized how they had agreed upon yet another point...and yet let that fact remain as they had to know what this crazy stranger was talking about.

"It really is quite simple. And before you start indicating how this fact is convenient so that those standing across the divide from yourselves will be able to understand it, at which point I will not say another word, I suggest you listen and learn," I told them as I walked down the line until I reached the end and sat down upon a large boulder to address the two separate factions, which unknowingly had formed into one group in order to hear my reasoning.

"Unless I miss my guess, your two groups formed over differences both stated as well as perceived," I began to the agreement of a number of nodding heads. "The only problem is that you obviously did not take it far enough," I continued to their surprise. "Let's take you Dissenters for example; you formed your group because you all were of the same mind and thus *had* to want identical things, right? But you're *not* all identical, so how could you *possibly* want all the same things?" I asked of the deepening silence. "Should a left-handed Dissenter feel certain issues to be as equally important as a right-handed Dissenter? If this was the case, where would you place a doorknob in order to be fair to all? If the Organization for Public Growth should ever decide to charge dues to belong to their faction, how should it be done? Would it be one rate per family or would a charge per person be equally fair? Obviously not," I answered them before they had the chance to do so, though I could see folks starting to think about my statements.

"So if we take this to its inevitable conclusion, a new faction of single OPG members would need to form while a group consisting of solely left-handed Dissenters would be splintering off from their main group to seek what *they* would see as their own demands being fairly met," I explained to a highly confused group of people who had been so certain that they were absolutely correct in all facets up until a few short moments ago. "Now if you take those left-handed Dissenters and realize how their taller members are being unfairly taken advantage of by their shorter brethren when it comes to any new construction of public buildings by the taller having to stoop to enter just because the shorter members see no reason to utilize additional lumber to make the doorways higher, well now you would have the needs of a faction of tall left-handed Dissenters not being met nor even hoped to be understood by their shorter *right-handed* friends! People, you have to agree with me that this two-party faction system of yours does not meet the needs of the community at all!" I argued at the top of my lungs while leading up to my grand conclusion. "What you need here—and what you should be demanding for the betterment of all—is Fractional Factions for everyone!"

When I stopped my ranting and raving, I expected to hear discussions from various sections of the audience claiming how what I had just said was the dumbest thing they had ever heard, or that I was a fool, or even laughter and derision. But I guarantee I never expected my pause to be met with the silence from several hundred villagers deeply lost in thought. I could see the nodding of heads as discussions did finally break out amongst small sections of the villagers; I even overheard one gentleman telling his friends, "The man has a point there."

How could this be? Don't these people understand sarcasm?

Trying once more to get their attention so as to debunk all which I had just declared, my voice could do little to overcome the cacophony of voices now raised in anger towards their fellow villagers. However, where there had been a mere two factions when I had arrived in town a short time ago, the crowd had now parted ways as they had separated into *six* separate groups of people busy arguing with whichever opposing party was the closest!

I tried to shout above the noise and explain how I had not been serious, yet my cries fell upon deaf ears. No matter how hard I tried to get them—to get *anyone* to see reason—my voice could not carry over the thunderous waves of noise being generated by folks who used to be kindhearted neighbors but had now morphed into a mob awash in a raucous sea of anger.

Begging any and all to see reason, I had just finished pointing out how they would need to work together to solve any of their problems when I felt a strong hand come to rest upon my leg. Fully expecting to have to defend myself, I quickly spun about only to face with the good Padre. Knowing how he could not be heard over the deafening roar, he emphatically motioned for me to come down off my perch upon the boulder.

Once I was back upon the ground, by cupping his hands together and placing them directly outside of my ear, I was able to understand what he was attempting to tell me. His message was short and emphatic.

"Follow me quickly if you wish to survive this day," was all he said as we fought out way through the sea of madness!

Village of the Damned

Recalling how the inside of a church was considered to be sanctuary and thinking this would be the best move I could make at this point, I followed Padre Bartholomew to the rear door of his small country chapel. Exhausted by my recent efforts, I asked that he allow me a few hours of rest within the confines of the church, after which I would be on my way. I saw no point in remaining, as it is a well-known fact of the road that arguing and screaming crowds do not take well to the passing of a hat; especially when that hat belonged to the fellow who had taken a village mired in mistrust and uncertainty and blown it up into absolute chaos in only a matter of minutes!

That is not an easy task to accomplish, even for me; although it does appear to be one of my natural talents.

Granting my request, Padre Bartholomew quickly shuffled me inside before anyone could take notice. Finding a comfortable spot in which to get some rest, I thanked him for his hospitality. Issuing a terse "You're welcome," he instructed me to bolt the door behind him. After which he was gone, returning to the fray while seeking to be a calming influence.

Despite the increase in the intensity of the screaming matches outside, I finally was able to fall into an uneasy sleep. How long I slept, I do not know, but what I *was* aware of upon a sudden awakening was a loud pounding upon the Church's back door! Cautiously sneaking up to the door, I ascertained that it was indeed Padre Bartholomew seeking entrance. Upon opening the door for him, the full intensity of the human storm taking place outside blasted into my ears until The Padre was inside and the closed door once again acted as a filter against all but the closest and loudest of screams.

Noticing how the nature of the cacophony outside had turned from the yelling of rage to screams of fright and pain, I asked him what had occurred.

"Knowing your heart as well as your good intentions, I cannot find fault in your actions this day," he replied (which sounded quite ominous to me). "Yet I am afraid that instead of being a calming influence as you desired, in reality you have stirred up a hornet's nest, for this village is on the verge of collapse!"

What I could hear of the noises coming from outside the Church—women's screams as heaven-knows what was happening to them to make them cry out in fear and pain while men's voices could be heard yelling "There goes one of them...get him!" These were accompanied by a lone, deep sobbing until it was replaced once again by screams of pain. Hell had come to Brackensburg this day and I was responsible.

Sensing the pain which I was feeling, Padre Bartholomew did his best to reassure me how this most definitely was not of my doing as the people of the town had already been teetering on the brink of mass insanity. It was a nice gesture on his part, yet his effort did nothing to dismiss my guilt.

Quickly taking stock of my possessions in the event that immediate flight should become necessary, I asked him what had happened while I slept to initiate this madness.

He replied that from what he could gather, it was the heads of the original two factions responsible for causing events to get out of control. "Seeing that they were about to lose many of their followers to newer factions and thus their positions of influence, the heads of both original groups started spreading lies about the other—lies which you could not possibly imagine," he said, not realizing how I could indeed imagine a lot. "It appears that once a lie was heard, another worse more depraved one would take its place until even family members were not immune to having terrible things said about them. The rumors of wives declared to be practicing witchcraft was soon to be outdone by the claims how certain daughters were less than pure; it was only a matter of time before it had gone too far and blows were struck!" he explained.

"It must have been The Devil himself who gave them both the same notion nearly simultaneously," he announced while pounding his fist against the wall. "While there are—or *were*—God-fearing people on both sides, there were also those in need of a cause to latch onto and serve as a source of self-worth," he surmised once he got his emotions back under control. "It was to these men that instructions were given to go out into the village and find members of the opposing faction...and beat them bloody!"

"My guess would be that the losers of those fights went home and came back with weapons seeking revenge," I conjectured to the sounds of the shattering of glass and breaking wood. The views of the deepening evening's darkness from the northwest church windows was suddenly replaced by a bright glow off in the distance. At the same moment, angry flames shot into the night sky visible from the windows facing both east and south.

"Oh my God...they're burning the homes!" Padre Bartholomew cried out in disbelief. Racing to the rear door of the church, our worse fears were realized as we gazed upon no less than half a dozen houses and cottages being consumed by flame. Amidst the fires bursting through the roofs and windows of those homes could be heard the high-pitched screams of those family members trapped inside!

The strong hands of Padre Bartholomew grabbed ahold of my tunic and held me back from rushing outside into the madness and trying to save anyone I could reach. "They are too far gone!" he lamented sadly as he pulled me back within the confines of the church. Struggling to get away from his grasp, I was determined to do whatever I could to alleviate some of the suffering which I felt responsible for going on right outside of our door, yet no matter how hard I fought he just held on more tightly. Striking him repeatedly as hard as I was able had no effect up on the death grip he held me in. With a cry I collapsed upon the floor, my tears mixing with his own upon the dust.

"Dylan…think!" he demanded. "You would not get twenty yards before you were recognized and probably killed!"

"And am I to do *nothing* then?" I asked between sobs while peering up at him through tear-filled eyes. "I cannot sit here and listen to the results of my mis-guided actions and do—nothing!" I yelled in order to be heard above the sound of a building collapsing close by.

Finally releasing his hold upon me, he said "If you truly wish to help, then bolt the door when I leave and don't open it for anyone besides myself." Before I could stop him he had gone back out into the madness. Following his instructions, I slammed the bolt home and went to check upon the front one as well. I had just returned to wait at the back door when I heard a knock followed by the muffled voice of the Padre telling me to open the door.

Opening it just wide enough to allow for his considerable bulk to enter, I slammed the door behind him and rammed home the bolt before I noticed that he was not alone. The forms of two small terrified little girls clung to either side of him, their dirt and soot smudged faces peering rapidly about as if totally lost amidst the hell being unleashed outside. When they saw me, they fought to burrow even deeper inside his comforting arms.

"Girls, this is Dylan, the man I told you about who is going to help us," he told them as he gently pried himself free of their grasps. "Dylan, this is Rhianna and *this* is Annika," he said as he placed their hands within mine. "Keep them here with you. Hide them if need be but make certain that you re-bolt the door and wait for me to return," he instructed as once more he made for the door.

Whispering to him that I have no experience with children, he smiled. "Hold them in your arms, quietly sing to them or tell them a happy story, and if you must, shed a tear with them; but try not to let them see fear in you," he instructed, and then he was gone.

The moment when I returned to where the girls were cowering against the wall they instinctively rushed into my arms, initially taking me by surprise. Fighting the tension which I felt flowing through my body, I was able to relax which I am certain the girls could sense. I asked them again for their names, their small squeaky voices replying between sobs. I began to hum an old song which I remembered from when I was a boy about a teacup and an old crow. Before long we were quietly singing it together in an effort for each of us to stay brave. The youngest of the two, Annika, was actually beginning to doze when once again I heard a rapping on the door followed by the voice of Padre Bartholomew. Placing her in the arms of her sister, and promising how I would be right back, I quickly opened the door to admit the Padre with three *more* children in tow. Pausing only briefly to introduce me to the young brothers Joseph and Jamie as well as an older girl Ashlye, once more he was gone out into the night.

Hearing adult voices outside for the first time, I moved the children back further into the shadows inside the church away from any firelight streaming through the windows. Placing them in Ashlye's hands, I went off in search of anything I could use as a weapon should it become necessary. Finding a candlestick that would do nicely, I went to stand guard beside the doorway and waited. Straining my ears in order to hear any voices outside, I actually found myself smiling amidst the destruction taking place around us as I heard the voices of these brave little children quietly singing our song once again.

It wasn't long before three more visits by Padre Bartholomew swelled the ranks of the children to a total of thirteen terrified little ones. I was introduced to the tear-stained faces of Ryleigh, Sydnie, Ethan, Kaden, Shylie, Ashlynn, Stephanie, and Maxin. One more appearance by Padre Bartholomew brought in tow Jack, Ivy, and Anthony; there were now sixteen small ones to be kept safe and be responsible for.

After this last arrival, he did not go back out right away. When I asked him about it, he grimly replied how there were no longer any more children remaining to be brought in.

The acrid pall of smoke from the burning buildings hung heavily in the air outside to an extent that it was beginning to even seep into the confines of the church. Breathing heavily from his excursions out into the murky air, Padre Bartholomew asked me to go into his private chambers and gather some cloth to make masks to tie around the faces of the children while he rested a bit.

Upon returning, I set about fitting the children for their masks, when I noticed him slumped heavily upon the floor, his chest heaving as if gasping for breath. I had managed to retain a bit of water in my flask; in spite of his wishing to keep it for the children, I insisted that he finish it himself. Preparing to sneak into the madness outside in search of more, it was when I asked him where there was some to be found that he said such a trip would not be necessary. I could find plenty outside of the village proper when I led the children away to safety!

Indicating how I had counted on just such a move and when would he be ready to go, I was in for the shock of my life when he informed me how he would not be coming with us. "It is you and you alone whom these little ones will be looking to for deliverance from this place," he told me readily. "I cannot go with you."

"In heaven's name, why can you not travel with us?" I asked, both concerned for his safety as well as fearful of the responsibility he was placing upon me.

"It is in heaven's name that I remain behind," he indicated as he offered me his hand.

"Come with us, I beg you!" I pleaded while holding firmly onto his hand and refusing to let go.

He just smiled at me—a man who was almost certainly going to his death *smiled*! "I am afraid that I cannot do, My Friend" he replied as he gently but firmly removed my grip one finger at a time. Having looked into his eyes, I did not offer any resistance. "Perhaps I can yet get some, even a small few to see reason and escape the madness that pervades outside this night. I can only hope…and try," he offered, the smile still retained upon his face yet the life and light with which he had spoken to me earlier had now left his eyes only to be replaced by a dull uncertainty. "Besides," he quipped as he opened the door to the screams and the madness outside "a shepherd never leaves his flock."

And with that he was gone.

The firelight dancing from flames unchecked throughout Brackensburg poured through the windows of the chapel to reflect upon the terrified faces of the children. They did not understand any of what was happening around them—as if it were truly understandable at all. What they did know is that their worlds had broken apart from happy times into very scary scenes being played out directly outside and there was no one to comfort them or hold them in familiar arms while quietly promising them how everything would be all right. For all I knew, they may have witnessed parents or family members lying dead in the street as they were hustled through the burning village by the heroic efforts of one Padre Bartholomew determined to save at least those members of his flock as he could.

At times of confusion and fear, it is inherent for a small child to look to the closest adult for guidance and shelter; whether I liked it or not, I could feel their eyes upon me pleading to somehow make all this go away.

Upon me!

It must have been divine intervention which took over my mind that night, for I immediately organized them into pairs, the youngest the direct responsibility of the oldest in the pair. I found a good length of stout rope which I instructed them all to keep ahold of. I made them promise to keep their eyes down and hold onto the rope with all the strength which they had. "I will lead us out of here to where it is safe," I promised them. "But you have to be strong now. Can you do that for me?" I asked each of them while waiting until I got their pledge before moving on to the next. "Keep your eyes upon the feet of the child in front of you, and I want you to repeat saying your name once you hear the child before you in line say theirs. We are going to get each and every one of you to safety, but you must promise to listen to your older partner. As soon as we can get to where the noise goes away, I will tell you some stories." I placed them along the rope, with Ashlye bringing up the rear with instructions to keep the others moving along in front of her.

Uncertain as to the shortest route out of the town to safety in the fields beyond, I began to feel a growing panic within—until I felt the tapping of a small hand upon my shoulder. Turning about, despite the mask covering most of her face, I instantly recognized the form of Stephanie.

"I beg your pardon, Sir," she said, her voice quivering in fear. "But I cannot remember laying eyes upon you prior to this day. Are you not from our village?"

When I admitted as how I had arrived just this morning, she offered "Should you wish to tell me where you need us to go, I can help direct you there."

Never was offered help more desperately needed...or more appreciated.

Informing them to wait inside the safety of The Church, I slowly opened the door. Seeing no immediate threat outside, I took hold of my end of the rope and we began our journey through hell.

Amidst the choking smoke and ash covering our unprotected skin, I followed the directions of one very brave young lady. How she was able to keep her bearings amidst the blinding grey intersperced with patches of angry red, I have no idea. But I certainly was thankful that she could.

Upon reaching the edge of the town, we began to feel some small degree of safety. Telling them to take off their masks as the air had cleared of the choking smoke, we were soon able to hear a most welcome sound. The babbling of a small brook as it ran over the rocks and stones was music to our ears. Stopping to rest, we drank while filling the few containers we had for later.

Having put the horrors of the death and destruction they had witnessed far behind them, the children's emotions burst forth with cries and wails painful to behold. Try as I might, there was no comforting them at this point. Even Stephanie was lost within the visions of a savage hell filling her mind which no child should ever witness!

Feeling panic in that I appeared to be losing them at this point, while unsure of what to do next, I began to sing the song which had helped lead us to safety. At first, mine was the only voice which could be heard mixed with the pitiful sounds of anguished little ones. No matter that no one followed my lead, I continued to sing it over and over until—much to my delight—I began to hear tiny voices sniffling the words of the tune. It took some time, but with the two older girls Ashlye and Stephanie walking amongst the smaller children adding whatever comfort as could be given, we became a brave little band once again.

Gathering them all about me, I told them a short tale to take their minds elsewhere. Heartbroken, yet feeling somewhat refreshed, we began our journey once again.

THE ROAD TO NOWHERE LEADS EVERYWHERE

Sixteen children I had counted in the Chapel, and sixteen children now gathered to rest once more about me in the tall grass amidst the chirping night insects as we had left the world of noise and fear far enough behind to begin to feel safe. Giving them a few moments to catch their breath, I remembered the instructions which Padre Bartholomew had given me on how to find the protection of the local Magistrate and his soldiers. Making certain that our pairs were still together, we started once more off into the dark of the night. True to my word, I began to weave tales of small woodland creatures or brave Knights and dragons for the children to keep their attention. Between rest stops when I counted heads and encouraged some of the bravest children I would ever meet, we walked all through the night. I actually got them to *sing* out their names; when it came time for me to do the same, I always did so in a screeching voice so off-key that before long they were doing their best to impersonate me to the sounds of scattered giggling up and down the line.

I have never been happier to hear laughter from any audience I have ever had!

As the sun began to rise the next morning, we could just make out the outline of our destination, the walls belonging to the castle of the Earl of Brighton, several leagues distant. It wasn't long before the aromas of breakfast being prepared in the castle kitchens wafted in our direction, causing exhausted little legs to pick up speed they never knew they had left.

If there was any doubt among the sentries manning the gate of my need for an audience with the Earl, the sight of the exhausted children slumped together (still in their original pairs I am proud to say) lent credence to an unbelievable tale they were hearing. After seeing to the care and feeding of the children, I was immediately ushered into the presence of The Earl to whom I proceeded to share the events of the past 24 hours. I answered his pointed questions to the best of my ability, yet there was one which I found I could muster not even the barest of answers to so as to clarify his misgivings: What could *possibly* have caused the entire population of Brackensburg to lose their collective minds?

Riders were dispatched to Brackensburg to verify my tale; they returned hours later with faces grim to behold. Despite praises heaped upon myself by The Earl for my part in getting the children to safety, I could not linger in his hospitality longer than a few hours to get some badly needed sleep. Provisioned with food and water, I said goodbye to the children before taking my leave. For the sake of my own sanity I had to get away from there and begin to try to forget the events I had experienced. No matter how hard I tried, nor which manner of desperation I employed, I never ever could!

I never did tell The Earl my name before I departed.

It is said that when the soldiers sent by the Earl to investigate my claims had arrived at the village, these battle-hardened veteran troops wept at the sight of the dead bodies lying scattered throughout. In one bloody night, nearly the entire population of Brackensburg had been decimated. There were a few survivors found; the blank stares upon their faces indicated a madness which could never be cured. An act of kindness from the soldier's blades freed them from their bonds of insanity, and now even more blood flowed upon the streets of Brackensburg.

A large communal grave was dug. The Earl decreed that as the villagers had allowed insignificant petty differences to cause them to take each other's lives, they would spend eternity mingled together in the ground never to be separated again—truer poetic justice was never issued!

Before the soldiers left, the crackling of fires could be heard emanating from every home and house of business which did not yet lie in ruins. The Earl had decreed that Brackensburg would be razed to the ground, its evil stench cleansed through the purity of fire. For months, regular patrols were dispatched in an effort to make certain how no one was trying to live upon those grounds. There would be no attempt to rebuild the village whose name would always signify a madness which had brought neighbor to fight neighbor, and brothers to kill brothers.

Yet, upon the edge of the roadway where the town had once stood, was placed a marker dedicated to the bravery of Padre Bartholomew, an unknown traveling Teller-of-Tales, and 16 courageous children who survived the night when an entire town lost their minds, their souls, and their lives.

Holiday Outt

I have heard in my travels how freezing to death can actually be a fairly pleasant way to die. You just roll over and go to permanent sleep. I am here to testify this is not the case, as the pain of cramping muscles or incessant shivering and shaking is *far* from pleasant!

Wearing every piece of clothing I owned did no good to battle the freezing cold which chilled me all the way to the bone. I gave up the idea of trying to light a fire, as any wood I could find still sticking out from the deepening blanket of snow was too wet. Huddled down in the darkness with my back against a fir tree with my two blankets wrapped tightly around me was the best I could do. And if the freezing cold wasn't bad enough, the swirling winds would constantly do their best to force freshly-fallen snow directly into my nose making each breath more difficult than the last. The part where you supposedly go to sleep? The numbness emanating from my fingers and feet kept any thoughts of peace and rest *far* away.

Oh yeah—that, and the howling of wolves off in the distance made certain how I would find no sleep this night.

What a way to spend The Holiday Eve! I should be enjoying the evening with friends and friends of friends perched near a roaring fire, my belly full of all the traditional feasting treasures with a peaceful smile of contentment pasted upon my face. The smile I wore this night wasn't pasted; it was *frozen* in place! What had started out as a light dusting of gentle snow made for a nice traveling companion as I walked my way south towards the town of New Market. Having never been anywhere near this territory previously, I had no idea just how long I had to travel; no less than half a dozen people I had encountered had assured me that it wasn't far. Being no stranger to sleeping outside during my travels, I thought nothing of having to do so once again should it prove to be a longer journey than expected.

By mid-afternoon, just as the road began to snake between what turned out to be the trees of a mighty forest, the flakes were starting to grow larger while falling much faster, the ever-increasing wind whipping them about making it nearly impossible to see more than a few feet in any direction. As the storm began to build in its intensity, the light-hearted jaunt with which I had begun my trek soon morphed into a muscle-tiring trudge through piles of deep drifting snow in places up to my waist as minutes became hours in my mind, all the while hoping how the town of New Market was just around the next bend. The deepening gloom of the coming of night made attempting to continue to follow what little I could still see of the frozen roadway impossible. I looked about in order to spy some manner of shelter in which to try to get a fire started, but the wind had made certain that all ground surface was covered by the increasingly heavy snowfall. Failing to find any open ground, I did my best by bundling up under the large fir tree for protection from the wind in an attempt to wait out this blizzard.

It did not take long for the freshly-fallen snow to completely obliterate any indication of where my tracks leading to my harborage had been. Ice began to build up around my mouth and nose from where my breath was beginning to freeze, indicating how the temperature was falling even further. I tried to crawl under the snow in an effort to retain what little body heat I had; a good idea if my clothing wasn't already wet and drawing any warmth I could maintain out of my hastily dug burrow to be dissipated into the howling winds. With no food, no dry clothes, nor any way to get a fire going, I realized that in all probability, I would not survive to see the light of day—should there prove to be any.

Growing very tired, I fought every attempt which my now heavy eyelids made to close for even a few seconds. In my weakened state, even one minute's peace would end up in eternity as I would never wake up again.

It must have been the howling winds playing one last trick upon my mind as I could almost imagine that I heard someone whistling a familiar up-tempo traditional Holiday song off in the distance. How *anyone* could be out in these conditions in such good spirits as to be whistling was beyond the comprehension of my foggy mind, and yet there could be no doubt as to the validity of the scenario as the steadily-increasing level of the tune was unmistakable. Using the last resources of energy which I could muster, I forced my protesting body up and out of my snowy crypt in faint hopes of attracting the attentions of the traveler and gain their aid. The reasoning side of what was left of my mind knew there was no way that I could signal anyone more than a mere few feet away due to the howling of the winds and the blinding snows, yet the stubborn side of my personality refused to give into an inevitable death without one last-ditch fight.

With all of my strength in one final push, my head finally cleared the last boundary of snow and I was able to see beyond my blanket of white into the gloom beyond!

To my absolute amazement, I could make out the shadowy figure of a rather large man facing my direction only several feet away, his hands resting upon his bent knee almost as if he had been waiting for me to escape my bonds. In spite of the unceasing tempest blowing about us, I found that I could hear his voice quite clearly.

"It appears that you could use some help, My Friend," he announced in a voice which indicated I had nothing to fear from this man. Quite the contrary, for I could swear I could discern a light heart and amiable nature in his tone. Barely able to speak, I did my best to answer, yet all I could rasp was some unrecognizable attempt at words.

"I'll take that as a yes," he answered while approaching closer. "Let's get you out of that hole and warmed up a bit, shall we?" He bent down to help me regain my feet. It soon became apparent that in spite of my best efforts, my weakened condition made certain I could not muster the strength to stand. I felt rather than saw two strong hands reach underneath my arms as with incredible strength he was able to lift my dead-weight from my burrow and bring me to stand on my two wobbly feet. Leaning against him for support, we were able to maneuver my numb and hopelessly shivering body a short way closer to the roadway. After what seemed to me to be an eternity, he announced that he was going to set me down to sit on a stretch of log still uncovered by the snow.

"You just set there for a spell," he instructed. "But keep your feet and legs moving up and down to get rid of that numbness or else you'll freeze for good; I'm going to find a spot to get a bit of a fire going."

Somehow, I was able to stammer my response about wet wood and impossible to get a fire going in this blizzard.

Setting down a large pack in the snow beside me, he gave a knowing chuckle as he proceeded to untie a bundle from its top. "It becomes a lot easier if you carry dry wood and tree moss *with* you," he laughed as he took the bundle and set out to find a better location for a fire. "Keep those feet moving," I was warned once again and in the blink of an eye he was gone.

Were it not for the sight of his pack by my feet and the fact that I was sitting on that log, I may have begun to doubt my sanity and imagine that I was dreaming as I slipped out of the world of the living still bound in my snowy prison. I did as he instructed, while refusing to give into the pain that flooded by feet and legs. I looked about but could see no sign of my mysterious benefactor.

But what I could see off in the distance was the bright flickering of flame as a small fire was born and coaxed into life, despite the best efforts of the elements to bring it down. To my great surprise, I forced myself to my feet and began to slowly stagger about in a small circle making certain that I never lost sight of his pack perched near that log and became lost in the storm. Keeping my head bent over to follow the tracks left over from my previous circuit, I heard a crunching of snow indicating that my benefactor was returning.

"Well, look at you now," he exclaimed somewhat in amazement. "Back on your feet and all! Think you can walk with me a short way?" He effortlessly lifted what must have been the heavy pack onto his shoulders.

"Try and stop me," I croaked in response indicating both my strength of will as well as some well-documented stubbornness.

He must have read what passed as a smile upon my frozen face, for he began his happy laugh once again. "Now that's what I like…real spirit," he said as we began trudging through the drifts toward the promise of warmth from the flickering fire beyond. More than once he had to steady me as my gait became unsure or the wind grew in strength; yet that fire always increased closer as we fought through to its rosy glow. As we stumbled through drifts of snow as high as my chest, I inquired to whom did I owe the return of my life this night. His reply that he was known to many various peoples by numerous names, why bother to even choose one, left me even more confused by events swirling about me this night.

Somehow finding a spot where the snow had piled up less than anywhere in the immediate vicinity, he had cleaned away any significant residual amount and cleared a patch to the ground where his fire was now pushing out a most welcomed warmth. "Wind's blowing mostly from the north," he informed me as he sat his pack back down. "Sit on down as close as you can to the flames to get warm. Turn your back to the north to block out as much wind as you can. I'm going to go find some more wood to dry so we can keep this little blaze going. You got any dry clothes in that pack of yours?"

A shaking of my head indicated no, an answer he had apparently been expecting. "I didn't think so—it looks kind of light." He reached into his own pack and pulled out a good-sized length of fur as if from a bear or large wolf perhaps. "We'll have to do this one layer at a time," he announced while handing me the fur. "Here, wrap this around you after you take those wet blankets and hang them from that tree branch over the fire to dry," he told me as once again he disappeared into the storm.

I could feel some semblance of strength returning as if fed directly from the warmth of the fire I was basking in. Peering intently into the bright oranges and reds at the fire's core, it suddenly occurred to me that while I had seen him just moments ago, I could not picture in my minds-eye the face of my deliverer, nor offer any description of his countenance! I could recall a large man outfitted in a brightly-colored fur-lined cloak with long white fluffy beard speckled with snowflakes as well as describe the redness of his cheeks or the contrast of his high black boots against the deepening blanket of white. Yet the more intense my effort to recall his features, the picture within my mind's eye began to blur all the faster.

Most un-nerving for one who made his living by the power of the spoken word indeed.

Quickly scrambling out of my soaking clothing, I wrapped my now dry and warm blankets around me followed by the fur as I hung the clothes up to dry. Settling back down in my spot, it occurred to me that while the storm continued to rage around me, when huddled close to the protection of the fire it seemed to lack any significant bite to it such as I remembered all too well. Soon my attention was drawn back into the magic of the fire.

Hearing the jostling of wood upon wood, I looked up from the hypnotic dancing of the flames to see that the stranger had returned, a large amount of wood in all manner of sizes in his arms which he placed around the fire to dry. Setting comfortably at the other side of the blaze, he asked if I were hungry.

Having paid such attention to all the other physical problems which I had been experiencing, it had completely slipped my mind—or my *stomach* to be exact—just how terribly famished I was. When I informed him how I had not eaten since yesterday…no, actually now the day before last, he reached into his pack from which he produced rye bread, parsnips, and cheese. "Far from a traditional Holiday feasting I'm afraid," he lamented. "But it will help get some strength back into you."

I was amazed how he was nearly apologetic by the fare set before me. "Oh Sir, this is without any question one of the best Holiday feasts I have in my memories and will most certainly remember it as such till the end of my days!" I gushed as I gladly reached for a hunk of bread he was offering. "Which, I may add, would have occurred *this* night if you had not come along and been my salvation," I included between bites while pointing the as of yet uneaten portion of my bread in his direction.

"You pay me too much kindness," the stranger protested in speech. The smile upon his face however indicated his appreciation of my sentiment. "I just happened along and saw a fellow traveler in need; could I have responded in any less a manner on this most special evening?" he asked in a way that left no need to respond.

"There is something which has been puzzling me above all else on this most remarkable of nights," I confided to him as he picked up more wood to place upon the fire. "How was it that you 'happened' along and were able to find me covered under a blanket of snow, as I was completely unobservable from not only the roadway if not a yard away? All other incredible events aside, the miracle of my salvation this night is proven if by no other means than that!" I ascertained to my attentive companion. "It was almost as if you were looking for me…" I stopped mid-sentence as my words resonated within my mind but could not clarify the significance nor their importance.

"Would it ease your mind if I told ye I was simply following your tracks in the snow?" he asked lightly.

Layered snow fell from my shoulders as I vigorously shook my head no. "Freshly falling snow was covering any tracks I could have left in a matter of mere moments," I told him knowingly. "There could not have been any sign of my previous passage to follow."

"There was for me," was all he would offer quietly.

I pressed him for further explanation yet was disappointed by his next statement which I considered at the time to be no additional clarification.

"Sometimes, it is not so difficult to find those who have strayed from the path and grown lost in this world," he told me with a twinkle in his eye—or was that just the flickering of the flames playing a trick on my tired eyes? "Regardless, My Friend, let us not question what manner of happenstance brought me to you this night but say simply it was a deed done and one well founded for your benefit as well as those as of yet unknown to you," he concluded while turning his attention once more towards the tending of the fire.

I took an opportunity in a break in the conversation to put back on what were my now dry and toasty-warm clothes. Wrapping myself in my blankets and the fur while taking my seat back at the fireside, I commented almost as an afterthought. "I will no longer inquire of the means of my salvation this night though I imagine I shall ponder them until the end of my days. Rather, I shall thank you for making the future of this simple Teller-of-Tales assured, and marvel at your belief how any future in question should impact others so greatly in the days to come."

Raising his head to gaze into my face, I could detect a look of genuine affection as the light from the fire danced upon his face. "I shall answer your confusion by asking you this simple question. Have you learned anything from the events of this day?"

To his great enjoyment, a light-hearted chuckling escaped with my answer. "While my chosen profession may label me a Fool in the eyes of some, I am by no means one in reality," I assured him, a hint of my exaggerated false self-worth evident in my tone. "Well Sir, for a start I have learned never again to travel without as heavy a load of dried wood upon my back as I can hope to carry. I will place no trust regarding the notion of distances between towns when uttered by peasants working in the fields when they have never been further than a league away from those fields in their lives—and above all I shall *never* question miracles which occur on Holiday evenings again."

The nodding of his head indicated that while there may be many more items of wisdom I shall take away from our meeting as I re-live it in the future, I must have stumbled upon what he had been insinuating with his question.

"So *much* to remember from just *one* evening," he observed. "And think how much more you could learn tomorrow, or the next day, or the day after that. So much wisdom being stored under that floppy hat of yours. Can you not see how all of that knowledge could be beneficial to others some day?" he asked as his eyes peered into mine.

Pausing to reflect upon his words, I answered how I could see me incorporating some newly-found wisdoms into my stories for future audiences.

"Oh, you will do more than that," I was told to my surprise. "So very *much* more!"

All I can say is that if confusion was heat I would have melted all the snow lying upon the ground for leagues in all directions. "You speak as if you can see events yet to occur, which swirl about my head like bluebirds circling a nest," I told him. Not the best of metaphors, though I did get my message across.

"Think not of bluebirds," he chuckled long and loudly. "Rather, pay attention to any *Robyns* which may cross your path. My Friend, there are those to whom this life is indeed a special gift to be measured not only in deeds done for their personal benefit but more-so in actions which mean so much more to others," he said almost lovingly. "A man is not placed upon this Earth to reap reward for selfish acts, but rather to learn from all which life has to offer and share new-found wisdom with others either by the spoken word or as examples to be followed by their actions. I see choices to be made destined to become deeds both great and yet terrible to behold in store for you!"

I could find no words to say other than to quip "Are your revelations more miracles attributed to this most amazing Holiday Eve?"

"You can say that if you'd like," was all he answered as he placed more wood upon the fire. Poking at the coals with the end of a stick, he never looked up from the fire as he declared with an almost casual air. "I know all about Brackensburg."

It was as if, for one distorted moment, all time stood perfectly still allowing for the demons which infested my dreams to rise up from the depths of the hell which I had helped create and tear into my very soul. It took several minutes until I could find my voice to quietly ask, "Were you there?"

His gaze had risen from his tending of the fire to peer directly into my eyes as he answered, "In a manner of speaking…yes."

"Then you know what I caused those poor people to do to each other?" I asked while tears began welling in my eyes only to freeze upon my face. I could feel the darkness of the surrounding night begin to gather around me as if squeezing the breath from my lungs. I tried to pick up a stick and throw it upon the fire but my shaking hands could neither grab nor hold it.

"Now, that I am *not* aware of," he replied in a quiet calming tone, "for what was done that night had been decided well *before* you arrived. Their madness was a natural response to their stupidity; you did little to add to that. The anger which they displayed towards their fellowman had been festering for quite some time. Believe me, the result would have been the same had you happened upon the scene or not," he tried to re-assure me to no avail.

The shaking back and forth of my head indicated that I was having no part of his opinion.

"I instigated all present that night," I argued with heavy sorrow in my voice. "I thought I was being inordinately clever when in reality all I was doing was pushing them to the brink!"

"Believe me, Son," he said as he came to sit down beside me and put his arm around my shoulders as a means of comforting me. "They were already there."

"So do you now claim to know what is in every man's heart?" I wondered incredulously.

"I know what was in yours," he announced much to my continuing disbelief.

"So if you know so damn much, why not share with me what you think you do?" I challenged him, my anger rising to the occasion.

"I know that you had no malice in your actions," he replied evenly, taking no apparent notice of my anger. "Think back...for the first time think back *honestly* to that night. Did you get involved in their tirades to goad them into a deeper madness, or were your motives an attempt at making them realize how foolish and dangerous their present line of thinking could become?"

He had me there. "I remember feeling how perhaps I could make them see reason if my words could be seen to carry even a portion of the foolishness which I saw but apparently they did not," I admitted to myself for perhaps the very first time.

"And did it work?" he wondered openly.

"If you know about that night, then you know how it did not!" I retorted as once more my anger came to the fore. I made to remove his arm about my shoulders, but my strength was no match for his and there it remained.

"Now why do you suppose that was—for does not humor often act as a balance for deeper darker emotions?" he now asked. Not waiting for me to agree with him, as I reluctantly was about to do, he continued on. "You tried to use one of your best talents and turn around what you saw as a critical need. Was it your fault how they would have nothing to do with it? Believe me, you were no instigator that evening causing the demise of the good people of Brackensburg, for by that point there were no longer any good people remaining!"

"Dylan, you tried to *help*. Is that something to be ashamed of and cursed by you until the end of your days? If you need more to ease your burden, would you like me to recite the names of the children you saved that night?" he asked. "I am certain that you can still hear the repetition over and over in your mind as you and you alone lead them to safety in the darkness. Remember this well," he said, pointing directly at my face as if he could bore through my skull and replace all of the guilt that I felt I owned. "If you had not been there, Brackensburg surely would have followed the path it was on and destroyed itself. You could do *nothing* to change that. The difference *you* made was in the lives of sixteen small children who live this day because of you. Without you, Dylan Ainsley, they would today be naught but smoke and ash. If you want a memory to cling to encompassing that damnable day, make it this...hear the children *sing!*"

One by one I called out their names in a reverence saved for only the bravest of heroes.

As if the lifting of an enormous weight from my heart and mind, his words finally broke through the veil which I had wrapped myself in so tightly since that evil night. I knew from that moment how I would be so constricted no more.

Sensing my change of heart, he gave me a long hug after which he rose and began settling his pack upon his back. "I must be off as daylight is but a few short hours away," he said while adjusting the straps upon his shoulders. "You may keep the fur. It is my Holiday gift to you."

Hearing how he was determined to keep traveling through what was left of the night, I became worried for his safety.

He appeared touched as well as appreciative of my concern for his welfare. "Believe me, Young Fellow, I've been in places much worse than this storm," he replied with his usual lilting laugh. "I'll see it through to New Market. It is only a bit over a league distant. Head for the sound of singing if you have a mind to travel in the morrow once you are strong enough."

Rising to my feet, I held him in a long embrace. I tried to thank him for all that he had done for me this night, but he dismissed my attempt at thanks as being unnecessary in the same manner as if swatting a fly.

"It's a good man before me I see," he told me with a wide smile upon his face, "and I take it as a kindness to be able to help out such as ye when your need becomes desperate. Sort of what I'm about." With a wave of goodbye he prepared to once again disappear into the shifting Holiday snow.

As the stranger began to walk away, I realized that in my hour of need I had failed in my attempt to gain the name of the man who had undoubtedly in many ways saved my life that night. "But I don't even know your name!" I called out to him as he began his departure.

Pausing mid-stride, the mysterious stranger to whom I owed so much turned to face me once again. A cryptic smile came to his face as he replied. "Oh, I believe that you do," was all he said as once again the blustering snows swallowed him as if he had never been there at all.

It was then I became aware how in spite of walking from the campsite to take his leave, he had left no tracks behind in the snow to mark his passage. Pondering this observation in conjunction with a number of almost countless miraculous occurrences which had led to my life having been saved that night, a smile of happiness mixed with wonder came over my face. Settling back into the comfort of the fire, I watched as the piece of burning parchment I had thrown in moments ago and which until this night had held captive my soul added new colors to the flames. Knowing with absolutely certainty that I now would survive this night to celebrate a most-joyous Holiday in New Market the next day, I concluded that yes— while I never would be able to offer a description of his features beyond this night as they quickly faded from all memory—I did *indeed* know his name.

On the Road Again

Leaving the town of New Market behind on the third morning after The Holiday, I did so with a spring in my step which had not been there for the longest time. After the nightmare at Brackensburg, I had felt I had overplayed my hand with my mortality and that it was sneaking up on me in an attempt to collect! Yet after my talk around the fire on Holiday Eve and the quasi-promises I had received regarding my future and all of the possibilities which I could, should, or would expect, I figure I have some pretty strong assurances that unless I can cram an awful lot of living into the next several weeks, I should be good for months, if not years to come.

I will refrain from chancing to purposely step out into the path of any runaway carriages I should happen upon to verify such a notion, however. The quality of luck in my life up to this point is not something to be tested regardless of veiled assurances. I do not need to meet any welcoming committee standing outside of the gates of Heaven with confused looks upon their faces as I am asked, "Is that *really* what you thought he meant?"

Now if I could only understand the dreams!

Ever since my strange encounter on Holiday Eve, I have been experiencing several recurring dreams every evening upon falling asleep which are as vivid as if they were actual occurrences. The first and strangest of all is this: I am standing upon the crest of a hill amongst many armed men, my body completely encased in armor with sword by my side. From perhaps half a league distant, I can see thousands of men with weapons raised running towards us as if to attack! From somewhere behind me, a voice asks of me, "What are your orders, Sir?"

Of me...this is asked of me!

The second dream is much more enjoyable.

I am outdoors amidst a large crowd of all manner of people, when I get the strangest feeling that someone is in need of my help. Glancing about the crowd, it is when I spy one particular figure that all of the other people vanish and I am left gazing into the face of the most beautiful woman I had ever seen. It is when I inquire if I could be of some help to her that I receive the most beautiful smile I can imagine. And then she is gone, and the dream ends.

I really like that second dream!

The people of New Market had been good to me as I walked away with not only some coin in my pocket but food and drink in my pack to make the journey to my next village down-right enjoyable—providing another winter blizzard is not lurking around the corner that is. It seems strange to be weighed down with so much, until I remembered that I have what must be at least ten *pounds* of wood and dried moss tied on top of my pack, Hey, I only *look* dumb and *act* stupid!

For a wandering Teller-of-Tales, The Holiday is a very good time to be at a larger town which New Market had proven to be. In most of the smaller villages in which I have plied my trade up to this point, the townsfolk would have only one day to celebrate the season before they would be required to be back at work. The clearing of woodlands to create additional fields for the growing of even more crops come next planting season or tending to the local Lord's flocks is indeed the life of a peasant in these times. Yet, in a more prosperous town like New Market, an entire class of people were to be found with more control over their lives than the common peasant could ever hope for. In the peasant world, if you do not work, you do not eat. Now if you were lucky enough to have been born into a merchant family for instance, your accumulated wealth over the years could provide for your food and comforts for quite a long time allowing for extended periods of celebrating—especially during this time of the year. No matter how much ale you have ingested, spending what could be days with the very same companions can get somewhat boring after a time. The promise of a good tale or two to pass the time is certainly something to treasure; which is surprisingly what they are willing to give up a small piece of if they like what they hear.

The first day in a new location is crucial to your success, for if word quickly spreads how a new Teller-of-Tales or troupe of entertainers are in town and are in reality quite good, it is not unheard of to have the owner of the local tavern approach you with the proposal of free room and board in return for utilizing their establishment to ply your trade. It is quite possible that I may have been able to extend my stay by a few additional days, if New Market had not been graced by the arrival of a group of minstrels with several very attractive young ladies in tow, for when it comes to the world of ale-befuddled wits, pretty girls beat out Tellers-of-Tales any day!

Why, oh why, did I have to be cursed with talent instead of good looks?

I did get some good points of reference from one of the young ladies regarding the towns along the general route I was planning on taking, just as I had shared my impressions of where I had visited which could be lucrative for them in which to ply their trade. It is a hard life being on the road; anything which can be shared by those who make their living on the highways and byways of The Realm is for the most part freely given to their fellow travelers. Unless they are Tellers-of-Tales by craft, in which case I usually send them to some make-believe town on the sands of The Channel with promise of riches beyond their wildest dreams!

THE ROAD TO NOWHERE LEADS EVERYWHERE

If they are dumb enough to believe that someone who tells stories for a living would share information with them which could result with less money in my own purse, they have no business being on the road. I have encountered some individuals upon regular occasions in my travels and actually struck up friendships with them, probably because they understand as do I that the sharing of an ale and some tall tales of your experiences may be one thing but one's livelihood is nothing to be trifled with.

There are occasions when economic gains are not to be realized regardless of the superior level of talent of the Teller-of-Tales as some villages are just too poor to find the ready coin to be shared. Many of my fellow travelers carry rudimentary maps with such known locations marked in red color as warnings to plot out routes which will allow them to steer clear of these villages. As I own neither a map, nor any ink the color of red, I have been known to stay several days in such villages offering stories to the children of all ages—especially adult children of course—in exchange for a place to stay or perhaps a bowl of thin soup.

Where is it written that the poor are not to be given the opportunity to share a smile with their families when that may be all they have to look forward to for many a day? Unless perhaps it is to be found in bold letters upon the backs of certain maps splashed with red in the hands of mercenary bastards who have forgotten what it means to be so poor that you have nothing to share but your hunger!

I have lived without money for a great part of my life, so I know what a few hours of stories can do to take one's mind off the fact their children will be going to bed hungry yet again that night. What those sons of dogs with their precious maps don't understand is that when I finally take my leave from a town such as I have just described, I may do so with an empty purse, but I feel as if I were the richest man in the world.

I never will become wealthy by living this life which I love; such is not my purpose. If I had sought a life with the potential for wealth and easy living I would have remained as apprentice for The Artist, for in truth I never went without a scheduled meal when I lived under his roof. Then again, I would never have known the reward read in a grateful old woman's eyes as she offered a mug of weak cider as payment for a long hot day of chopping the wood which would guarantee how she would not freeze during the upcoming winter.

One meets quite a number of unforgettable characters as you travel from place to place; that is what truly makes this an interesting life worth pursuing. The Sheriff who proposed the fitting response to the clothes-less cur is someone whom I will never forget. The 16 children and Padre Bartholomew from Brackensburg will always be sources of my inspiration and I feel honored to be of what little service I was to those brave souls. Then there was this beautiful tavern girl who…um, better forget that one!

One man who I will always remember was a giant of a man who had decided to visit the tavern where I was working just the other night (in which town this occurred I cannot recall, as there have been quite a number of them). Apparently, the ales which he had been downing since earlier that afternoon decided to do his talking for him, as he found it very amusing to interrupt the story which I was trying to tell the other patrons every few minutes with comments until any hope at maintaining continuity was completely lost. When several of the other men trying to listen to my tale voiced their displeasure, he quickly became very belligerent and threatened them with imminent bodily harm.

Taking a bit of a chance, when I was able to regain this man's attention, I asked if he was a man of action or simply full of enough hot air to be able to fill the sails of a ship and push it along in even the calmest of seas? Getting over his surprise at being talked to in such a manner from a fellow shorter and much less muscular, he turned towards me with malice evident in his eyes. Talking quickly, I inquired if he was man enough to accept a challenge from one such as me? "Prove to the entire tavern that you are a better man than I, and I will personally buy you your drinks for the rest of the evening," I told him, making certain that I maintained eye contact with him throughout. Naturally the fickle audience began goading him into accepting whatever manner of test I should propose. Realizing that he could not refuse my challenge without losing face, he roared how there was nothing on this earth which he could not best the likes of me in, so bring on this contest—after which he would deal with me once he had won!

"Very well, I will keep this simple so that even you will be able to understand the parameters, My Large Muscular Friend," I announced to the howls of the audience which he did not appreciate in the least. As I figured that he could only kill me once, I commenced to describe the nature of my contest.

"What I propose is a test of both physical strength as well as strength of willpower," I told him, while looking up at his face as he towered over me. "Do you think that you have what it takes to beat the likes of me?"

Growling how on his worst day he could destroy me at anything that I could suggest, he told me to make my challenge and hurry up about it!

"Very well. It is my contention I can remain under water longer than you," I told him as if confident I considered him to be little true competition. "I see a rather large bucket over by the fire—one large enough for even your gigantic head I would imagine." I pointed to the bucket. "I will even let you go first," I said as the bucket was retrieved by the owner of the tavern who figured rightfully so how this was a night to be discussed over many an ale during the coming days.

"If the audience would be so kind as to count off the time, we can begin," I announced after which the man plunged his head into the bucket full of water while holding onto its sides with the two massive hands which he was certain would be rendering me at the very least unconscious when this little display was completed. Enjoying the spectacle unfolding before them, the audience proceeded to count.

At the number of forty-five having been reached, I could tell how he was forcing every second he could manage. When sixty-six was announced, his shaking hands could no longer hold him under as with a great intake of breath, he lurched out from the bucket, water cascading onto the floor where he stood fighting to catch his breath.

"You did very well, My Friend. Sixty-six was your total," I told him.

"Good enough for second place I'll warrant."

Confident that he would end up the victor, he downed a full mug of ale in one gulp. Slamming the empty mug onto the top of the bar, he pointed to the bucket while growling for me to do my best.

Walking over to where the bucket remained, I exaggerated my movements as I placed it right at the edge of the bar, then moved it several inches further to the left. Standing with chin in hand as if studying the placement, I ended up putting it back in exactly the spot it had been prior. Finally satisfied how all was in readiness, I proceeded to take a seat on the floor directly under where the bucket was perched.

You could hear a pin drop as I instructed the audience to begin their count. Figuring that they would be too surprised to offer a count, I began to do so myself. Unable to understand what I was doing, my fellow contestant bellowed how I was cheating, which I ignored while informing the audience that they were not counting.

It was when the giant, beside himself with anger, accused me of cheating once again that I calmly informed him how I was doing no such thing. "The bet was to determine which of us could remain under water the longest," I explained in between reaching the number seventy-two, after which I stopped counting and announced that I had indeed been victorious. "You lasted until sixty-six…a fine attempt to be sure. I, however made it to seventy-two and thus have obviously won!"

Before he had a chance to offer a dispute, I proceeded to point out that the challenge was to remain *under* water. "I cannot help it if you decided to put your fool head *into* the bucket, for I never said *in* water—the instructions were to remain *under* it. The bucket is above me and thus I must be underneath it. Even you must agree that I have been victorious," I informed him with a grin upon my face and an offered ale in my hand.

You could see him working out in his head just what the instructions to the challenge had been, until he burst out in deep prolonged laughter.

"Stranger, I must bow to your convictions," he announced as he took the ale from my hand. "You have indeed bested me this day." Afterwards, he vowed to keep his silence as I finished with my tale. The evening ended with him shaking my hand while still chuckling over the nature of my victory.

I did very well that night, as I went to sleep with nearly a full purse.

The next morning when I left my room with my belongings in hand so as to step back out onto the road once again, he was waiting for me by the door. More than a little concerned as to his intentions, I was *very* relieved to discover that he was indeed waiting for me—to offer to walk with me, as we were going in the same direction for some miles.

In this way, I made a friend of a man whose name I discovered to be William Whitestone, a farmer by trade in a town little more than a day's journey to the south. I found his company to be most welcome, for walking long distances with only yourself to speak with can become very boring indeed.

I asked him to tell me about his home, which he did in such detail that I began to wonder if he would be taking my job of Telling Tales from me and I would be forced to try my hand at farming. The hours flew by as he described many of the people who called his village home so well until I felt that I had known them for years. I became so impressed with his enthusiasm for the life he described that when it came time for me to take the left fork in the road and he the right, I threw caution to the wind and maintained our walk together. While it may have ultimately been my decision to make, it was his words which convinced me to accompany him for the entire journey and try my luck in the village known as Arlington Green.

Ales Well That Ends Well

Gladly accepting a coin from one of the last people remaining in the village square due to the lateness of the hour, I sat back down upon one of the benches by the fire lit especially for my performance. I was about to investigate what I hoped to be new-found bounty in my hat tossed in by an appreciative audience, when I heard words near and dear to my heart. "Would you care for a drink, My Young Friend? Your throat must be in need of some ale after so long a dissertation." Stashing away my hat for later, I glanced up to see a mug being offered by a man who I recognized as having been enjoying his second evening of amazing stories.

Would he be offering me a drink if he had not?

"I thank you for your kindness, stranger," I nodded while reaching for the gift of libation. "Incessant talking does work up quite the thirst," I admitted as I took the first sip of a very fine brew.

"It is not often when an audience is treated to *three* grand tales in the same evening," he observed smiling. "What your take is for the evening residing in yonder hat was well earned I assure you. I don't believe that I have ever spent an evening with these folks with nary a word even *whispered* among them! To say that you had captured their interest and attention would be a proper understatement."

"I am indebted to your graciousness, My Good Sir," I thanked him again while soaking in every word of his praise. "To hear how one's efforts are appreciated, especially in *my* line of work, warms the heart indeed. Perhaps, even more so than this most marvelous ale," I told him while emptying the mug of its contents.

Setting his own mug down on the bench next to me, he took the empty one from my hand. "Well then, perhaps if you are not too anxious to be off to your room at the inn or wherever you may be sleeping this evening, you would favor me with some short conversation—accompanied by another mug that is."

Having learned early in life some hard lessons when I called Perilous Alley home, one can never be too careful on the road—especially when it is known one has a fresh supply of coins in his hat. I have been known to be a good judge of character, and in this man I found no need for concern. By the glow of the firelight, I determined him to be in his early forties, with shoulder-length dark hair beginning to show a hint of grey. His clothing as well as his mannerisms indicated an educated man. His hands were neither deeply marked by years of constant toil nor soft and free of callouses; I assumed him potentially to be of the merchant class.

Recognizing the depths of my thirst and not very anxious to take up residence in the stables where I would be spending the night—if I did not get caught and forcefully removed that is—I was glad to take him up on his offer. Putting some additional wood on the fire as he left to have the innkeeper refill our mugs, I took the opportunity to slip the contents of my hat into my pocket with some into my shoe none-the-less.

Apparently, some of the lessons of the road are not easily ignored regardless of impressions!

The evening's breeze began to play upon the fire for the flames danced as if to a silent music all their own when the kind stranger returned, his hands holding two full mugs and a fresh loaf of bread. "I took the liberty of bringing you something to eat," he said as he offered both the cup and loaf to my eagerly awaiting hands. "At the rate which you are devouring the bread, I see that I did not err." He laughed while re-taking his place upon the bench.

As it is impolite to speak with your mouth full, the vigorous nodding of my head indicated how he not erred in the slightest.

"So tell me, my Young Fellow, is the world of a traveling Teller-of-Tales in reality as adventurous as it sounds?" he wondered, patiently waiting for me to finish my mouthful of bread before I offered up an answer.

"Well, Sir, there are times when I believe that years ago my hat must have been too tightly set upon my head for even thinking of making this life my own," I told him with a light-hearted laugh soon matched by his own. "If one enjoys being drenched by the rains, baked by the summer sun, or frozen by the winter's storms with hunger and thirst as your only traveling companions—unless one is being chased away in the early morning hours by the owners of stables or even worse the Magistrate's guards—then I can say with no shadow of doubt how this is the life for you."

Peering at my face as if capable of reading more than my words, he eventually asked "Were you not able to surmise that these hardships would be your experience before undertaking such a life?"

"In spite of what you may see before you, My Good Sir, I assure you I am not so feeble-minded," I answered with a smile to signify that umbrage was neither meant nor taken. "I knew that it was not an easy life I was choosing by any means, and yet I don't believe any of us—regardless of manner of livelihood nor station in life—can predict with any certainty the degree of difficulty which life has in store for us," I said to the accompanying nodding of his head in agreement.

"Very well said, Young Fellow," he replied. "And still I wonder. As there is intelligence that I see hiding behind those eyes of yours even in the darkness, what was it about this life which you found so attractive as to give up your former existence all the while cognizant of the hardships both real and imagined to be faced?"

A good question I must admit. I found myself enjoying my conversation with this man to the same degree as the ones I used to have with The Artist as we worked late into the night.

"Have you wandered much in your time, Sir?" I asked eventually.

"While I have done *some* traveling when I was younger, I am afraid that it was not to the extent nor in a manner similar to your experiences," he admitted, his curiosity evident in his tone. "Why do you ask?"

"Well Sir, perhaps then you would realize how much there is to be gained by a lifestyle such as mine," I explained between sips of my rapidly disappearing ale. "I am as free as the breeze to roam where I will, I have had a lifetime of experiences which I never could have even dreamed of had I remained where I was, and I certainly would not have met some outstanding and highly notable folks such as yourself had I never taken to the road. While it may have been a bit 'harsher' than I would have hoped for, I can easily attest to the rewards which I have accrued. And by that, I do not indicate those rewards to be simply a matter of coin for my pockets."

"Or for your shoes as well?" he inquired to the sounds of hearty laughter. "Be not concerned—your secret is safe with me." He must have read the discomfort upon my face in being discovered. "If I may, I have noticed how you have not utilized the word 'home' in any description of your previous experience," he observed, once again studying my face for any response. "Was the road a means of running away from your former life to find something better, perhaps?"

I probably took longer to answer his question than I should, but then I was weighing just how I was going to reply. "You have been very kind to me, and I wish you to know I appreciate the food and drink and especially the company, but that is a subject I do not broach," I told him firmly. "I am no refugee from the law nor do I have anyone looking for me." This was the truth to *some* degree, for as The Artist's apprentice, the law knew just where to find us when it came time to receive their payoffs.

Rising as to take my leave, I was stayed by his hand upon my shoulder. "Accept my apologies, I beg you, for I assure you I meant no disrespect. Perhaps with one more ale in hand you can find it within yourself to forgive me for being so direct?" he asked hopefully.

With my full agreement as well as my blessing, he left to fetch yet another drink. I found myself wondering about this man; while I recognized him from the previous night's audience, curiosity grew within me as to why he would have returned to be listening to my stories again this night. What was his interest in a simple Teller-of-Tales? While I felt no concern for any ulterior motives which he may harbor, I found it somewhat disconcerting to be talking about myself so readily to a stranger. I have always masked myself behind personal walls meant to keep the world at distance. I found it easier to deal with life this way since the loss of my parents at so young an age. I was determined to change the direction of our discussion upon his return; perhaps he did not hit so far off the mark with his question after all, for freedom comes in many guises.

I thanked him once again as yet another mug of ale found its way into my hand.

"We have spoken naught but about me this entire time," I began as he sat back down. "Tell me about yourself, for all I know of you is that you are generous and are an avid listener to tales woven by Yours Truly."

"Avid is an interesting word," he replied, "for it indicates a deep need to have such a desire met."

It was my turn to study him now as I pondered his answer to my last comment. "And yet avid is exactly the word I choose, or else why would you have been in the audience not only this night but the last as well?" I inquired. "Returning to suffer through the possibility that you should hear naught but a familiar tale repeated and thus grow bored indicates more than a passing interest in an evening of entertainment, My Good Sir."

I did my best to appear casual while inwardly craving an answer to my observation.

Took him by surprise with that one!

"If you wish to be less noticeable, try not to sit in the same spot two nights in a row," I offered with a hint of superiority.

"Would it offend you and your considerable powers of observation if I told you I wished to see if you had noticed?" he inquired with knitted eyebrows.

Why should my noticing his attendance be of any possible consequence? This was turning out to be a very interesting conversation indeed. "Now that would depend on who you are and what you are about," I answered with a hint of irritability thrown in for effect.

"A fair answer," he agreed with a grin. "As for my name, it is Raymond and I reside in yon Manor House with the Lady of Arlington Green and the other members of her Staff." He pointed in the general direction of the large house upon the far hill which I had noticed immediately upon arriving in the village.

How could you not?

"So—hobnobbing with the 'Divine Right' crowd, are you?" I quipped in jest.

Apparently, it was my turn to have broached a subject of which *he* had strong feelings about. Does this make the score one to one?

"Divine Right!" he scoffed, as if the mere saying of the word resulted in spitting the sour taste from his mouth. "What is 'Divine Right' but an invention of men whose only interests are to have a fully laden table at breakfast provided by the sweat and labor of those whom he sees fit to keep in near slavery and thus assure that his dinner table is even more opulent? What do they care if sickness or famine run rampant through the villages and towns under their jurisdiction?" he demanded.

Fortunately, he did not wait for an answer as I had none to offer, but rather continued his tirade. "The population becomes decimated—their troops burn out the pestilence with fire—and another generation of peasants and indentured servants re-plant and rebuild; unfortunately for them, in that order! For what importance would such a tyrant place upon the needs of the poor souls who labor in his fields?" he asked, the growl in his voice indicative of his opinion on this matter. "Their purpose is only to provide food for his table or add to the wealth of his family. What would he care if they had to live out in the elements for weeks before basic shelters could be erected once the fields had been tended?"

I found myself highly impressed by the passion which his voice did imply. "If that is the case Sir, then how is it that the Realm could thrive unless certain men be endowed with rights and privileges by The Creator Himself for the benefit of its society?"

Some of the fire had subsided from his eyes, his voice calmer and more dignified. "Son, a God just and loving would never appoint men flawed by greed and malice to oversee the welfare of his people. That responsibility—nay, that RIGHT—should be *earned* by the 'Noble-Born' each and every day. They reap the benefits of the toils and the tears of their people, the luxuries upon which they measure their greatness are bestowed upon them by those who work their fields in sickness regardless of the weather. It is those privileged few who need to answer to their people and look out for their welfare. You have that," he emphasized by pointing at me, "and you will have a country which does not just subsist…it flourishes!"

"Don't let the local Lord hear you speak so," I cautioned him with a whisper once I had placed my hand upon his shoulder and brought him close for secrecy. "You may find yourself in the stocks…or worse."

A smile came to his face. "I am genuinely touched by your concern," he told me while giving my shoulder a pat. "I don't think I have any fears along those lines," he laughed as he rose to take his leave.

For several moments he looked down upon me as if studying me once again. "I wonder if I may ask upon you for a favor?" he queried. "The Lady of Arlington Green is a great lover of the arts—music, singing, the telling of a good story. If you will, I shall arrange an audience tomorrow following supper for all who reside there. In exchange, you shall enjoy a most excellent dinner, have a roof over your head for the night as well as even more coin in your pockets...or your shoes if you'd like." He spoke with a most heartfelt smile. "Would you be interested in such a venture?"

While interested in his proposal, Nobility was a class of individuals I had always made it my business to steer as clear of as possible. I had seen what happens to those who raise the ire of the local Lord, their pitiful bodies broken in the stocks or hanging from the battlements of their opulent castles.

Naturally, I was a bit skeptical.

"This Lady of your Manor; what is she like?" I asked so as to gain information and help decide to accept his offer to return to the road in the morning.

"As far as being a member of a noble family, she is actually quite tolerable," he said while smiling. "If this should give you any indication of her qualities, we have not had a defection from our Staff in over three years. That must say something for her I would imagine."

I thought it meant quite a lot and indicated to him my thoughts.

"Do not get me wrong," he said as if to clarify any qualms I had which may keep me from accepting his invitation. "While being in truth a woman with a kind heart, she was born with a contentious spirit and a need to overcome any challenge," he admitted freely. "I do believe that she would take a shine to you, My Friend."

"And if she did not?" I inquired.

"Don't worry," he said, the flickering flames of the dying fire revealed his wide grin as if he was enjoying a secret joke known only to himself. "You would know it if she did not."

Intrigued, I answered in the affirmative before he had the opportunity of rethinking his offer.

Appearing most pleased with my agreement, he shook my hand firmly with the remnants of the dying fire revealing his smiling eyes. "Excellent! Make your way to the Manor before sundown," he instructed while dousing the fire with the contents of his mug.

I found myself pondering my good fortune as we parted company. Before the gloom of the night swallowed him from sight, he called back. "Oh. I figured that the horses could use a good night sleep, so I arranged with the innkeeper for you to have a room for the night—that is, if you want it of course."

Yeah Buddy!

All Manor of Foolishness

True to my word, I arrived outside the Manor the next evening just as the sun was setting. As I was about to have dinner with Nobility, I was wearing my best clothing. That is to say, the *new* clothing which I had bought that morning with some of the new-found wealth gleaned from the grateful audience of the night before. I had gone all out in order to make a good impression, even to the point of visiting the local river for a badly needed bath.

The Manor House itself was surrounded by a high wall made of tight-fitting stone with a heavy wooden door its only entrance from the outside. Pausing to straighten myself out, I was just reaching to pound the heavy doorknocker when with a slight squeaking of the hinges, the door opened to reveal a man I took to be somewhere in his fifties with sword upon his hip. I was about to explain to him why I was here when he informed me that he knew who I was, and would I please follow him. Not waiting to see if I was accompanying him, he turned and made his way across the courtyard, leaving me to close the weight of the door on my own. Eager to satisfy my innate curiosity, I took the opportunity to look about as I followed.

The main section of the Manor House itself stood two stories tall with several attached outbuildings of a single story. One feature which I noted right away were the many windows adorning the exterior walls; excellent for warmth and sunlight, but a definite drawback should the house ever need to be defended.

The building to my right revealed itself to be the stables if not from the sounds of the horses within then definitely from their smells—something I was somewhat an expert on, having spent many a night in a dry stall to keep out of the weather. I was just beginning to quicken my step in an effort to catch up to my greeter when he saved me the trouble by tripping over the tip of his sword; had he not been able to right himself by grabbing a convenient post for the tying off of a horse's reins, he would have undoubtedly fallen flat upon his face. Reaching out to help him gain his stability, I was informed in no uncertain terms that such an effort would not be necessary, after which he once more lost his footing and this time did *indeed* fall flat on his face!

Doing my best to squelch a desire at laughter, I helped him to his feet before he could offer any resistance. While waiting as he brushed the dirt from his clothes, I heard a voice behind me say "I see that you've met our resident Knight, Sir Preston Monroe." Once I was certain that Sir Preston had regained his footing, I turned to the owner of the voice; he was a young man whom I estimated to be about the same age as I.

It was there that any semblance between the two of us ended. A full head taller, I deemed him to be a working man by the size of his strong arms and broad shoulders. This, plus the fact that he was exiting the stables while brushing God-knows-what from his tunic, brought me to this inevitable conclusion. In this way I met Stable-Master Bryce Willis, whose broad grin indicated someone I felt I would have been able to call friend.

"Oh, pay no attention to old Sir Preston," he told me while offering me his hand. "He does things like that quite often."

"And just what are Sir Preston's responsibilities here at The Manor?" I asked out of curiosity.

"Sir Preston is the Knight of the Manor and as such is in charge of security," I was told. Before I could question what he had said, he nodded to indicate how he was being in earnest.

"I take it that security is not a major concern at this time," I concluded once Sir Preston was out of earshot.

"Fortunately, that is the case," he offered, accompanied by a shaking of his head. "You must be the Teller-of-Tales from the village. Going to entertain us with a great tale after dinner I understand."

"I don't know about a *great* tale," I said "but there is to be a tale or two none-the-less. My name is Dylan and I'm not actually from the village; just passing through as it were."

"So I gathered," was all that he said while opening the door to the Manor House for me as Sir Preston was nowhere to be found. Taking his leave to go prepare for dinner, I was left to my own devices; I soon found myself wandering along the corridor gazing at paintings of previous generations of Dukes of Arlington Green.

"Not very much to look at, are they?" the voice belonging to my drinking companion of the previous evening wondered as he made his way down the hall. Stopping to warmly greet me, he glanced at the painting which I had been studying at the time. "Have you given any thought to which tale we are to be treated to after dinner?" he wondered as he offered me a glass of a very nice wine.

"Actually, I have spent all afternoon doing just that," I said. "I wanted to make certain the one which I chose to be perfectly appropriate for the occasion."

"Care to enlighten me regarding your choice?" he asked, intrigued as we proceeded to slowly walk further up the corridor.

"I imagine it to be one you may find fascinating," I replied while leaving just enough time to peak his interest before I continued. "I don't believe you have heard it's like before. I call it 'The Tale of the Overly Clever Duke and The Highly-Observant Teller-of-Tales'. Do you think that it might be worthwhile in its telling?" I asked with a devil-may-care grin upon my face.

The echoes of our footsteps decreased by exactly half as he came to an abrupt halt while I continued walking as if nothing noteworthy had just occurred. Pausing my own steps as if in relation to his lack of movement, my exasperatingly slow turning about to gaze back at my stationary companion was perfectly timed. The complete lack of surprise registering upon my face had been practiced earlier this afternoon in the reflection of the river until I got it perfect. Throw in a tilt of my head with a slight increase in the blinking of my eyes, and I believe that I got it just right.

"I apologize, My Lord, but I'm afraid I am not readily versed in how to behave in the company of Nobility," I called back to him with a tone indicating my sincere insincerity. "I do hope that I have not offended you in any manner."

Now if I had been able to tell him this *without* a smug grin upon my face! I had to give him credit. While my statement must have taken him by surprise, he was doing a marvelous job of not revealing this fact. Instead, he casually sipped his wine as he stood gazing upon one of the paintings hanging upon the wall. Indicating that I should join him, he waited until I was standing right beside him before he began to explain himself.

"This particular Gentleman whose image you see before you upon yon wall is my Great-Great Grandfather Desmond," he began to instruct me while continuing to casually sip his wine with an air of indifference equal to my own efforts. "He is famous for a great many things," he continued with an honest pride in his voice "yet he is most famous for—or *infamous*, if the truth be known—his handling of what became known as 'The Night of the Intolerably Insufferable Fable-Flinger'. It is said by all but the subject of the exercise that the placement of the sharpened stake which brought about the successful conclusion of hostilities was nothing short of poetic." Shifting his attention from the painting, then back to Yours Truly, he casually noted with just the hint of a smile "Of course, it did require the gentleman to utilize a large pillow to allow him to sit for many a day afterwards."

"Shall we declare a truce?" he inquired eventually, obviously proud of his improvisational efforts.

Taking a few additional moments as if studying the image upon the wall—then turning to face The Duke—then the painting—then The Duke once again, with a nodding of my head I concluded that such would be a prudent course of action.

"Should you desire to remove a place setting from the dinner table, I do believe that you would do a very credible job of creating and sharing your own after-dinner story for the listening pleasure of your family, My Lord," I concluded as a praise-worthy peace offering.

"Thus speaks the Master to the Apprentice," he replied, obviously enjoying this bantering as much as I. "Been doing a little inquiring with the Townsfolk, have you?" he asked without asking.

"Wouldn't you, Your Grace?" I wondered without wondering.

"Quite," was all he said as we began our walk once again. Later, I was to find out that the figure in the painting was actually a distant second cousin named Darby, whose claim to fame was as a keeper of pigeons.

Pausing outside of a double set of wooden doors, The Duke placed his hand upon my shoulder. "While there are times and places where formal titles are necessary for a person in my position, my home is not such a place, nor are my guests invited to my private dinner table expected to cling to such formalities," he told me. "If you must, 'Sir' will do nicely with 'My Lady' reserved for The Duchess."

I thanked him for his kindness by indicating how I had no formal education regarding how to address the Noble-Born.

"Then you are a lucky man indeed," he quipped as he opened the door to the Manor Dining Room and motioned for me to enter.

Like a sharp slap in the face, the amazing aromas of what their Chef had prepared for dinner that evening hit me before I even made it into the room. The last time I had been able to virtually pull flavor from the very air was…actually, I had never been even close to performing such a feat, as I had never been in the vicinity of such a feast before. I honestly hope that I was not drooling as I took my place at the table where The Duke had indicated.

Taking my cue from the rest of my dinner companions, we all remained standing until The Duke returned with The Duchess on his arm. Seating her at his right hand, he remained standing in order to introduce all there to the guest for the evening—meaning me. As he sat, we all sat, after which the other diners went around the table offering me greetings. In this manner I was introduced to The Duchess first as was proper—I do hope that I bowed low enough. While I could see her honest and heart-felt smile as a means of welcoming me, I could also detect how she was intently peering at me as if attempting to determine the true nature of the fellow seated before her. Had I more time, I would be doing the same, for I could see that the intellect of The Duke was equally matched by that of his smaller yet equally formidable wife. Her introduction was followed by the woman to her left, whose name Nanny Kaye indicated her obvious responsibilities within The Manor. Next to her was seated The Duke's youngest son, thirteen-year-old Brandon, his older brother by only three years, Tremain, (Tre for short) to his immediate left and at the end of the table…or he was at least as long as they did not start arguing. The familiar face of Bryce grinned at me from my right while the familiar face of Sir Preston glared at me from my left. The place open between The Duke and Sir Preston was reserved for The Chef who was busy with last minute details regarding dinner but would be joining us shortly.

Enjoying some pre-dinner libations, when I was not taking part in the conversation, I could not stop glancing about the dining area. Even throughout a most marvelous dinner, I could not help but steal a furtive look around the room. Not finding what I had been seeking, my face must have revealed a degree of my confusion to draw the attention of The Duchess.

"You seem ill at ease, Mister Ainsley," The Duchess observed as if she had been studying me intently—which is probably what I would have been doing were our roles reversed.

"I must bow to your powers of observation, My Lady," I answered truthfully. "It is not often that I am welcomed into a home such as yours. I am loath to inadvertently do or say something which may be deemed to be inappropriate or blatantly incorrect by either yourself or your husband. I am genuinely moved by the gracious invitation which you have extended to me; to put blemish upon it in any way could not be further from my heart."

"Have you spent any time with Sir Preston as of yet?" she inquired.

"I have had the pleasure as I arrived this afternoon, My Lady," I replied while wondering as to her meaning.

"Then be at ease. I do believe there is very little which you could do that could top the antics of our Dear Friend, even if you tried," she observed candidly. The wisp of a smile indicated to me either the depth of her love for the old Knight or her weariness at granting him her repeated indulgences.

I thanked her for her kindness—then immediately proceeded to do what must have attracted her attention in the first place.

"MISTER AINSLEY...what on earth are you *doing?*" she demanded in a voice I would imagine had previously been exclusively reserved for Sir Preston. "Is there something in *particular* which you are searching for amidst the shadows of this room? I am certain that more candles could be procured so as to make said search a success and we could get on with our meal!"

"Again, a thousand apologies My Lady," I found myself groveling. "I am merely looking for the presence of the myriad of servants whom I assumed to be toiling behind these walls for the benefit of you and your family."

"Oh, we have none of those," she replied with a sense of pride in her tone. "We don't believe in them," she continued to explain and thus gain my admiration. "We have a handful of Staff Members whom you see seated about the table to assist us, but you will find no serfs nor slaves either in these walls nor outside of them anywhere in Arlington Green."

"It appears that our guest has spent far too long outside in the sun this day if the lovely shade of red upon his face is any indication," I overheard a snickering Tre whisper behind his hand to an equally giggling Brandon.

This exchange did not go unnoticed as The Duke wondered aloud if there was something that the boys would like to add to the conversation to be shared by all.

Now it was Tre's opportunity to share my embarrassment, or so I surmised by the rosy color of *his* cheeks, as well as his attempt at stammering out an answer that would show respect for his father and his guest.

"If I may, Sir," I interjected while stealing a glance over to the boys, "your Son Tre was just commenting to his Brother how healthy I appear due to all of my time spent upon the road out amongst the sunshine."

Okay, some may call my explanation a lie. I prefer the term "embellishment of the truth". Either way, I had just thrown two drowning boys a rope—now to tug on it just a little.

"Yes, Young Masters, a man can most certainly use his time in traveling throughout this great country of ours to grow strong in *many* ways." I shared a look that indicated "You owe me one" which only they could see. "One would naturally expect the legs or body's general stamina to gain; this goes without saying," I continued while utilizing my best lecturing mannerisms and tone. "Yet you may be surprised to learn that it is a man's *senses* which outgrow any visible physical appearances which his body may outwardly indicate."

"Would you care to elaborate upon that statement, Mister Ainsley?" The Duchess asked, much to the chagrin of the two boys who probably felt they were being set up for a fall.

Responding how I would be delighted to do so, I turned my chair to face the boys directly.

"Now boys—picture for a moment that you are walking amidst a grand forest stretching for miles in all directions as the sun begins to slowly sink into the west. What would you imagine is one of the first thoughts going through your head when you realize that the shadows of the trees are lengthening and you will be spending the night alone deep in the woods, with all manner of animals both large and small your only companions?" I asked Tre directly.

"Naturally you would be intent upon starting a fire," he replied with an air of self-induced superiority.

"Excellent! That would be just what your focus should be. And why do you suppose that would be, Master Brandon?"

Being the younger of the two and not as well versed in the art of subtlety, Brandon fought for an answer accompanied by the rolling of the eyes of his older and *much* wiser brother; an act which did not go unnoticed by his father at the far end of the table.

"Perhaps you would care to elaborate upon your answer for the benefit of us all, and not just your younger and less *experienced* brother?" The Duke suggested to Tre—who must have been siting too close to the fire as those darn cheeks of his were beginning to turn red yet again!

An outburst of what had to be snickering quickly turned into a bout of exaggerated coughing as all eyes turned in the direction of Bryce, who took the opportunity to just happen to hide behind his dinner napkin in an effort to capture a potential escaping sneeze.

Such lovely manners.

"Well, as it is the end of the day, I would be looking at starting a fire to be able to cook my dinner I would imagine," Tre replied, looking to me for agreement.

If he was searching for an ally, he wasn't about to get off that easily. I inquired as to what manner of dinner he would be expecting to be preparing.

"Whatever I had been able to catch during the day, I suppose," he answered, the beginnings of doubt creeping into his voice.

"Ah...but you are traveling and thus eager to arrive at the next village as soon as possible in an effort at earning your living. Setting traps and waiting for a capture is not really an option," I explained. "As you are wandering through the local Magistrate's woods, hunting of any substantial game is punishable by death if they are so inclined, so that is not really an option either. And as it is mid-summer, any food not heavily preserved with salt or pickling would be rancid before you were ready to eat it."

An irritated Tre pointed out that I had never mentioned how it was summertime.

A casual me replied how he had never bothered to ask.

Apparently, Bryce's cold was catching as now it was the Chef's turn to break out in his own coughing fit as he gathered up the dishes and utensils from our completed dinner.

"Brandon, let's see if we can help out your brother here," I suggested as a means at evening out the playing field. "If we assume for a moment that we had taken the opportunity at gathering edible nuts and berries during the day when it was still light enough to find them, which would require a sharp sense of sight—another of those senses I was referring to earlier—and had some manner of food not requiring cooking, why else do you suppose we would be wanting to get a fire started?"

If anyone had noticed that I was slyly pointing to my eye, it was not mentioned—and I am certain that Tre would have mentioned it most emphatically if he had!

"So that we could see in the dark?" he offered sheepishly.

"Correct! Very good, My Young Sir. We would want to be able to see in the dark," I clapped my hands for emphasis. "Can you imagine any other reasons for us wanting to have a fire going before nightfall?" I inquired, while making sure he saw me looking directly towards the fire.

"To try to stay warm?" he asked, but with more confidence and conviction this time.

"Correct again...very good answer," I praised him once more.

"But you said it was summertime!" Tre protested adamantly, only to be reprimanded by *both* of his parents regarding what they saw as bad manners. Looking down at the floor, he offered his apologies for his outburst.

"No offense taken, Young Sir," I assured him. "Sometimes such a resounding response indicates an over-directed sense of passion, nothing more."

Glancing in the direction of The Duchess, I couldn't help noticing a sense of confusion upon her face while trying to discern if I had just accepted an apology or brought his attitude down another notch. "You seem ill at ease, My Lady," I quipped with precisely her previous words.

Instantly her confusion turned to understanding; I got a nasty look for that one, but I could not have let such an opportunity go!

Eager to return to the discussion before I did anything additional to gain her wrath, I pointed out to Tre that yes, while it did indeed get very hot in the summertime during the day, at nighttime it could get surprisingly cold, especially when there was a strong breeze indicative of an impending storm.

Opening up the discussion now to the entire table, I asked if there was any other good reason why a fire would be advantageous to a traveler alone at night in the woods. Looking about a very quiet table, I could tell some serious thinking was taking place. With the exception of The Duke who was slumped back in his chair while enjoying the scene playing out before him, all were lost in thought until Sir Preston of all people gave the answer which I had been looking for when he said one simple word: safety!

"Leave it to a Knight to arrive at the optimum answer," I said, while nodding in his direction before addressing the boys once again.

THE ROAD TO NOWHERE LEADS EVERYWHERE

"One thing you will learn, My Young Masters, is that nature always seeks a balance. While there are many creatures who feast on those same nuts and berries in addition to plants, if their numbers increased out of proportion, soon that great forest would be eaten down to the roots and all would starve. That is why animals such as foxes, or bears, or even wolves hunt in order to survive."

"Dylan, have you ever seen a wolf?" Tre asked, his excitement open for all to see.

Inwardly I was smiling, for once again I had captured the interest of whom I figured to be the most difficult member of my audience unless one should consider The Duchess...and even she appeared to be hanging upon my every word.

"Have I seen a wolf, you ask? Thanks to God's good graces, I am happy to say that I have survived just such an experience," I told Tre much to his excitement. "I have not *seen* them often...but I have heard their mournful cries as the pack hunts in the dead of night more times than I care to recall. Believe me boys, should you be out in the woods at night, that is a sound which you will never forget!"

The lessening light from the dying fire in the hearth cast shadows throughout the room which the candles attempted to rectify but could not. Positioning the candles directly before me on the table so as to highlight my features in the gathering darkness, I set about to take my audience where they had never expected to go.

"Imagine for a moment that it is late at night," I began, taking the time to look everyone in the eye for effect. "You've been walking all day, and yes, it is summertime so the hot sun has pounded down upon you all day long mile by long mile so you are tired—more tired than you can ever remember. Knowing how you cannot keep your eyes from closing much longer, you put plenty of wood upon your fire. Build it high, so that it lasts most of the night," I advised through experience. "Setting your back to a tree so that nothing can strike you from behind, you curl up in your blanket. Wanting nothing more than to close your eyes, you keep them open for one more sweep of the surrounding woods in an attempt to reassure yourself that you are safe and will awaken the next morning to continue your journey."

"All too soon, the chirping of the crickets and bugs of the night complete their lullaby and your body relaxes, the pain in your legs from too much walking with not enough water subsides, and you wrap yourself in the deepest most beautiful sleep."

I could see a few heads begin to nod—time to rectify that!

Slapping my hand upon the table, I jumped up from my seat to exclaim "Suddenly, even through the fog of your weariness, you hear the sound of that which you dread: the wolf pack is on the hunt tonight…and they are close! By now, just like in this hearth, your fire has consumed nearly all of the wood you had provided earlier. Hopefully, you have been prudent enough to place extra within reach and can quickly rebuild it so as to provide a wall of flame, for that is your only defense. The small knife which you carry will do little to no good against the thick fur of *these* proven hunters."

I took a quick drink of wine to combat my dry throat and return to the tale, for I do not want to lose them at this point.

"The flame of your fire is just beginning to build once again and none too soon, yet you feel no comfort from the warmth of the flames as a cold-chill creeps up your spine, for the calls of the hunting pack are getting closer!" I began anew to my audience's delight. "Perhaps your scent has carried in the breeze and it is you whom they hunt this night?" I wondered aloud.

By this point, Brandon had gone to sit in the comforting embrace of his mother. Tre being the older of the two would have none of that; he had taken to sitting right next to his father, however. Bryce was scrunched forward as close as he could be to my side, as if this would help him to hear the tale all the sooner. Nanny Kaye sat completely motionless, the white of her knuckles evident even in the darkening room as she held her hands to her mouth. Chef had inadvertently picked up one of his carving knives and held it tightly in his hands, while Sir Preston sat nodding his head up and down as if in recollection of just such an event. Even The Duke had ceased his studying of those around the table to peer intently into my flame-enhanced features.

"Quickly you consider your options," I said while diving back into the tale. "*Very* quickly for time has run out and they are here. You can see their eyes reflected in the firelight; your stomach drops as you realize how they are all around you...you are surrounded! Flight is impossible, for they run much faster than you and you would not get far. Fight is the only option which you have, and while they have nearly all the advantages, you have the one making the difference this night good or ill. If you have not panicked and have your wits still about you, you have a very powerful weapon indeed."

"Dylan, in heaven's name, what would you possibly do?" Tre asked hardly daring to breathe.

Slowly I shook my head back and forth while telling him "It's not what *would* I do, Young Sir. It is what *did* I do, for I lived just this scenario not too long ago."

Shifting slightly in my chair so as to take the candlelight away from my facial features, I ever-so-slowly proceeded to roll up the right sleeve of the shirt I was wearing. Even in the muffled candlelight, like a bolt of lightning streaking across a blackened night sky, the pale-white pasty skin indicating the scar from the bite of a large animal stood out starkly against the rest of the sun-kissed skin of my forearm!

Reactions from around the table consisted mostly of sharp intakes of breath—The Duchess's was of such strength that it blew out the flame of the candle sitting before her on the table—causing her to flinch at its sudden disappearance and nearly knocking Brandon from her lap. Nanny

Kaye had to turn away for fear of fainting, while Chef's considerable bulk pushing down upon the table top so as to get a closer look nearly toppled the entire table over. Bryce indicated to me that was one nasty bite I had there, while The Duke was nearly bowled over by Tre's failing arms and legs as he could not reach the sanctuary of his father's chair fast enough. Sir Preston merely mumbled "My word," with all of the excitement of a hiccup. Asking him if he was not impressed, he simply turned to me and casually inquired if I wished to compare scars?

I could hear The Duchess comforting Brandon by telling him that I was here telling the story so I *must* have gotten away. It was when he asked her *how* that she could offer nothing for a response.

Taking a moment to assure Brandon—in addition to who knows else—that I did indeed survive, once the flames of the candles stopped flickering back and forth in reaction to the shaking of the table, I continued with my tale.

"Now, as Sir Preston will attest," I continued with measured tone, "when you are surrounded by those who mean you harm, you must do two things: narrow your field of fight, and then toss your caution to the winds and take your fight to the enemy and attack the biggest, baddest, boldest leader of the pack! For if you can take *him* down—and that can be a very big if—chances are the rest will leave you be."

"I had only a heartbeat to determine in which direction I would strike!" I told them as I peered about the table. "Pulling some of the flaming branches from my fire, I tossed them around in a semicircle so as to narrow that field of fight. There is very little which a full-grown wolf is afraid of. Fortunately for me, they are downright terrified of fire! Saving the stoutest flaming branch for myself as my only weapon, I gathered all of my courage and *charged* at that place in the surrounding trees where I judged the leader of the pack to be. Yelling as loudly as I possibly could as both a means to scare them as well as boost my courage, I attacked with only the flaming brand in my hand."

By this point I had taken to standing next to the table where all could see the deadly scenario played out in word as well as deed within the safety of The Duke's Dining Room.

"As quickly as I could, I flung that flame back and forth as I charged where I knew that hound from hell to be. Paying no attention to the growls surrounding me or the threats they signified, it was just as I felt his teeth latch onto my forearm and begin to rip into my flesh that I lashed out with the end of my branch directly into the face of the biggest blackest wolf I had ever seen! Sparks flew into the night and I knew my aim had been true. Where just a moment before I had faced a solid wall of death, the evening breeze carried with it the diminishing howl of a wolf in pain followed by…nothing! I could smell the aroma of burning fur, but there was no sign of its owner, nor the rest of the pack, for that matter. Not trusting to my good fortune, even before I dressed by bleeding arm, I immediately collected more wood nearby and built my fire even higher than before. The advancing light of the morning found me still vigilant, my back to my tree with plenty of flaming branches at my disposal."

"I guess it's ironic, but regardless of how tired you are proven to be, the cure for weariness is a good bout with a pack of hungry wolves," I observed, wrapping up my story.

"But Dylan, how did you know where the biggest wolf would be so as to know where to attack?" Tre wanted to know.

This was fortunate for me; for if he had not, then I would have had to bring this fact to their attention as this bit of information tied my effort complete.

"Well, Young Master, do you remember when earlier in the evening I said how traveling allows for the increase of the senses?" When he acknowledged that fact, I completed my night's work.

"From my earlier wanderings, I had taught myself to be able to tune my ability to hear to near perfection. In this manner, I could discern the deepest growl, the sharpness of breath, as well as the increased crackle of the underbrush to indicate the position of the largest and heaviest animal. Once that information was known, it just became a matter of gathering my bravery and fight as if my life depended on it. In this case, it most definitely did!"

More candles were lit as dark shadows were dispersed from the room; I could only assume that in some rooms they would not go out for the rest of the evening.

As the hour had grown late, it was time for the boys to be in bed. They emphatically thanked me for my most excellent tale—their words not mine—and hoped they could hear some more in the future. Thanking them for their kind words, they had almost made it out the door with Nanny Kaye when I called out to them "Remember, Young Sirs, if you should take any lesson from my tale this evening it is this: I…Hear…Everything!"

Funny, though he was across the room from what was still a dying fire, Tre's face once again turned a deep red as the meaning of my words was realized.

A Higher Hire

Being unfamiliar with the workings of a Noble household, I did not wish to offend. This fact, coupled with having spent the night in the most comfortable bed I had ever known, made me decide to remain there until summoned. It was after I awoke for the third time that I assumed they were unfamiliar with the workings of a Teller-of-Tales named Dylan and were not doing any summoning. Reluctantly, working my way out of that most wonderful bed, I once again dressed in the clothing which I had worn the previous evening.

They were all I owned without holes in them after all.

Doing my best to retrace my steps from the night before when I was shown to my room, I did an absolutely horrible job and never came close to where the Dining Room had to be located. I did however manage to find the kitchen just in time to meet Chef coming in from the outside with a basket full of fresh greens.

"Ah, the mighty hunter rises," he laughed while setting his burden down upon his prep table. "I was thinking that maybe you had risen early and left us without any entertainment for the evening, until I enlisted Tre to sneak into your room and see if you remained. I'm not trying to tell you your business you understand," he chuckled while handing me a cup of tea, "but I don't think your 'I can hear anything' line is going to work anymore."

"To tell you the truth, I'm rather surprised it did at all," I confided in the big man.

"I'd wager here comes a certain young man whose room remained well-lit all night long," he announced under his breath while pointing out the figure of Tre approaching from the direction of the hallway. From the rapidity of his step coupled with the grim look upon his face, I do believe I was about to be set upon by a wolf-pack of one.

"You made me look like a fool last night!" he announced angrily, once he had gotten to within a foot of my face. "I guarantee that will never happen again."

"I'm sorry Young Master, but could you repeat that?" I asked, while cupping my hand around my ear as if to hear him all the better.

"I said that I will never be fooled agai—" was as far as he got, until with a scrunching of his face he realized that it indeed had just happened once again!

"I'll make a deal with you, My Young Friend," I offered. "Suppose neither of us takes the other for a fool. I certainly know that you are worthy of all considerations, a bright young man with an even brighter future," I explained readily. "As I am obviously back upon the road by this time tomorrow, shall we call a truce for the evening?" I inquired while offering him my hand.

"I will take your hand if just to prove that I am as good a man as yourself," he replied somewhat reluctantly. "As for your future plans? I suggest you have words with my father. He is looking for you even as we speak."

My curiosity piqued, I inquired if he should know to what end his father wished to converse with me.

Grabbing an apple as he made his way outside, his reply of "Why yes, of course I do," followed by silence let me know that while we may understand each other somewhat better, the game was indeed still on.

Gaining an insight from Chef of where The Duke generally was to be found this time of day and more importantly how to get there, I thanked him for his kindness and hurried off before I could forget the directions I had just been given. While such a statement may sound foolish in nature, it was an absolute truth. A dirt road winding its way through a forest can be easily followed and thus I can generally get to where I wish to be… eventually. But navigating a path through the ins and outs of the residence of Nobility can be another thing altogether. For all I knew, one inadvertent slip of the tongue or a trespass of any sort and I could be experiencing the teachings of Dear Great-Great Grandfather Desmond first hand!

Passing single doors, and double doors, as well as *closed* doors, I finally arrived at what I believed to be *the* door to The Duke's Study, where I paused to straighten myself somewhat before knocking. I had actually contemplated looking for Bryce to see if I could borrow some clothes. I immediately tossed that notion aside as foolish even for me. Better to be seen in clothes familiar from the evening previous than in those at least four sizes too large.

My rapping upon the door was answered by none other than Sir Preston. Giving me the once-over from head to toe, his dour expression did not change. Whether this meant he did not approve of what he saw, I could not tell. Asking if he should remain, The Duke said that would not be necessary, but did ask if he would please go find The Duchess and have her join us.

Once the door had closed behind him, The Duke let out the smallest of quiet laughs.

"You must forgive Sir Preston, My Boy," he said as he motioned for me to take a seat across from where he was sitting behind one of the biggest desks I had ever seen. "He means well and has served me faithfully these many years."

"Was he a big fan of jousting, Sir?" I inquired while imagining what the end of a lance could do to one's head after years of sudden meetings.

Putting down the papers he had been attending too, The Duke sat back in his chair with folded hands as if studying me yet again. "You have a definite air of irreverence about you, don't you?" he observed, indicating to me how he had gathered my meaning precisely.

"And yet I mean no harm or disrespect, I assure you, Sir." I did my best to explain myself. "I will admit that I make jests at the expense of others too often...many times when I do not even realize having done so—and yet I have no malice for the objects of the exercise. It is just my way."

Suddenly fearful that I may have inadvertently said something I should not have since my arrival, I quickly offered how I held him and his family in the highest regard and hoped that I did not say anything out of turn or which he had found disrespectful.

"You may wish to ask *me* that very question, Mister Ainsley," The Duchess announced as she stepped into the room. From the icy tone of her voice, I almost expected to spy Sir Preston lurking out in the hallway with sword drawn in search of my innards. The questing look I gave The Duke was simply met with a shrug of his shoulders and raising of his eyebrows; he purposely was being no help in the least.

Rising quickly to my feet, I hesitated to ask her to please qualify her remark yet did so readily while offering to make amends for any affront which I may have inadvertently committed.

It was some of the best groveling I had done in a long time.

Surprisingly she appeared almost disappointed with my replies. "And here I thought you to be more difficult to maneuver," she reluctantly admitted while coming over to stand next to her husband. "What happened to the mighty hunter of last evening I wonder? Perhaps with you it is more difficult to know if truth and fable have *any* common ground?"

she observed as if purposely goading me. "What a pity. Apparently there is more 'story' than 'Teller' in you."

I knew I would regret this, but there are times when I just cannot help myself.

Without saying a word, I simply raised my *left* sleeve to reveal the unmistakable scars from the teeth of a very large animal bright upon the otherwise sun-darkened skin of *that* forearm!

The Duke's eyes grew wide with amazement as he gazed upon the wounds of my outstretched arm. The Duchess on the other hand turned white as the color drained from her face, her shock not as easily concealed as that of her husband. It was now *her* turn to offer apologies for her words.

Motioning for me to re-take my seat, I could read new-found respect in the eyes of The Duke. "Then the tale of the wolf attack was worse than you would have had us believe?" he asked barely above a whisper while quickly providing a chair for The Duchess to sit in before she collapsed upon the floor.

"Were that I could say it was not," I replied bravely while hesitating before I added "and yet surprisingly at the same time, I must agree that it *was* not."

It certainly was nice to see how Nobility could become as confused as us common folk. Sharing expressions indicating how one was as lost as the other, it was The Duke who broached the subject for them both.

"Dylan, I find myself at a loss from your explanation. Was there indeed truth to your tale or not?" he questioned.

"Oh yes Sir, there indeed was," I re-assured them both.

"And you were bitten on this arm as well while fighting for your very life?" The Duchess asked in awe.

"No, My Lady," was all that I replied.

Once again, expressions of total confusion were shared.

"Dylan, did you have a run in with wolves during your travels or did you not?" The Duke asked directly.

"I can answer with all honesty that I did indeed, Sir."

"And in the process one or more of the wolves bit you on both arms?" The Duchess inquired in an attempt to gain clarity.

"No, My Lady," was my curt reply.

From the looks I was now getting, I began to wonder if I would very shortly be escorted out the front door at the end of Sir Preston's sword.

"Dylan, listen *very* carefully!" The Duke cautioned, the tone in his voice indicating a rising level of frustration which he was not used to experiencing. "Did you or did you *not* get bitten on both arms by a wolf during your travels?" he demanded.

"No Sir, I did not," I answered honestly.

"You never did have an encounter with any wolves, did you Mister Ainsley?" This was more of a statement of condemnation rather than a question from The Duchess.

"Yes My Lady, I did," I told her factually.

Before Sir Preston could be summoned, I explained my answers. Yes, I did experience wolves, and yes, I did suffer an attack leading to wounds; but no, I did not get bitten twice by any wolf.

Fire now flew from the eyes of The Duchess, as she snapped "So, you resort to lying directly to our faces, in our own house, after we invited you to be our guest!"

"No My Lady, I did not, nor would I ever," I replied much to her chagrin. "While I may be a Teller-of-Tales—and a darn good one if I may add, my craft requires me to embellish the truth upon occasion to heighten the effects of the story. Lying, on the other hand ,is a question of morality. What I have shared with you this day resulted in no cheating or stealing or my taking advantage of you for my personal gain. Believe me, I know the difference," I assured them earnestly. "I hold you both in the highest personal regard and while I may have jested with you, I have not lied at all."

"Why you most certainly did. In fact, you just did so again! How can you claim otherwise?" The Duchess continued her tirade.

With my calmest Teller-of-Tales voice, I told her that I had not. Before she could protest I bid her "Think back My Lady: you indicated how my tale of last evening was potential fantasy. I neither denied nor disputed this fact; my only action was to raise my second sleeve to show you a bite upon my other arm. Not once did I claim it was given to me by a wolf—you *assumed* that to be the case, and I did not dispute it."

"While I am guilty of having led you on for too long of a time, for which you have my apologies, not once did my words form an actual lie."

I could see them both replaying the last few minutes out in their minds. Begrudgingly, The Duke admitted how I was right. The Duchess, however, was not ready to capitulate just yet I suppose.

Requiring further explanation, The Duke simply asked, "And the bite?"

"I received that courtesy of a Magistrate's hound who was capable of running just a bit faster than I," I informed The Duke…once again the truth.

"So you are a thief then!" The Duchess judged me as if the weight of her words justified her losing what she must have imagined to be a battle of wits.

"No, My Lady, I am not," I answered with indignity at the accusation. "And before you once again question my integrity, it was no act of thievery which earned me this 'reward', but rather the act of stopping one of his men from ravishing a poor peasant girl to pay the family debt. I do not go about displaying it readily, but I wear it with as much pride as the one upon my other arm none the less."

An uncomfortable silence permeated throughout the room until it was broken by The Duke who asked me an innocent enough question. "Do you play chess, Mister Ainsley?"

Taken aback by the inquiry, I answered that indeed yes, I loved to play.

"Apparently your game is not reserved for being played just upon a chessboard," he replied with the hint of a smile. "The Duchess loves a good match as well. From the events here today, I do believe that the two of you would play quite the spirited game."

"It is a pity that we shall never know the outcome of such a match," I offered, for I could sense the same in her as well.

"And now why would you assume that to be the case?" The Duke wondered as he glanced over at his wife while receiving just the hint of a nodding of her head.

"Your original invitation was to join you for an evening," I explained. "I did not expect to be granted a longer invitation." In truth, I found the inevitability of returning to the road less than desirable as all who reside here appeared to be earnest and of good character and manners. All had treated me well and with respect (at least I *think* Sir Preston did). But above all, I know for a fact I shall never sleep in so comfortable of a bed ever again.

"If that is truly the case, then please explain to The Duke as well as me how it is that you remain here at this late hour?" The Duchess inquired, some of her earlier fire missing from the tone of her voice.

"Temporary insanity, My Lady?" I offered with no grin upon my face, while inside I was laughing hysterically at my cleverness.

"*Finally* we agree on *something*!" the exasperated Duchess admitted. "I do believe that I *would* enjoy matching wits with you, Mister Ainsley," she said, regaining an overly-exaggerated sense of superiority meant to be obvious.

"My Lady, wasn't that what we have been doing just now?" I asked all pious and humble-like.

The Duke just sat back in his chair taking it all in. "Yep, a *very* spirited game indeed," was his opinion. Fortunately for me, his observation was made with a smile upon his face.

Refusing to look in my direction, The Duchess turned to The Duke. "Well, hurry up about it then before I change my mind!" he was told in a huff.

Refusing to get drawn into the battle, The Duke ignored his wife's demeanor and instead got to the matter at hand.

"Dylan, do you remember the other night when I questioned you about your home?" he asked, taking me completely by surprise. My answer to his question died on my lips as he continued. "You took umbrage with my asking, in the same manner as you were prepared to just now. I will not ask you why," he said while holding up his hand in an effort to stop what I was going to say. "Whatever reason you respond this way is for you to know, and you alone."

This time, I got in a spoken rebuttal before he was able to continue.

"Sir, with all due respect for yourself as well as The Duchess here, I fail to understand why this subject appears to be of some importance to you." I could sense my defense mode taking over as I became guarded with my responses as well as my emotions. Pain hurts less when it is blocked and thus felt on the outside, not allowed to penetrate into the softer inside where it could do the most damage after all. (Eventually I would learn that such a response also fails to allow one to fully love, but that is another story altogether).

Offering up an explanation for his line of questioning, The Duke said simply, "I ask you this because The Duchess and I would like to offer you an opportunity to make Arlington Green your home."

At that moment, I believe I somehow knew instinctively just how it would feel to have the tip of a lance smash into one's helmet during a joust. Head spinning, unable to concentrate as mind is obliterated, unable to discern if the breaths entering and escaping from your mouth are yours; your name lies upon the tip of your tongue yet eludes you at the moment. All of that sums up how I was responding to the question which I *think* I had just heard correctly.

"Sir...you will have to pardon me, but I am certain you would understand my confusion at this moment," I said as I fought within myself to clarify this situation. "I mean, with the exception of an occasionally great tale, as well as your sons having the opportunity to learn all kinds of new words from The Duchess as I win chess match after chess match, I fail to see any reasons for such an offer being made."

"That is because you did not allow me to finish," he lectured me as a Headmaster would a schoolboy.

'Okay Dylan' I thought to myself. *'Shut up. Listen to what he has to say, and then try to figure out what the hell he is talking about'.*

"For a while now, The Duchess and I have been debating the education which the boys are receiving. Learning the use of letters or the operation of mathematics are given concepts with direct conclusions," he explained. "Yet when it came for them to reason beyond the realm of yes and no or right and incorrect, we felt that they were floundering. In short, they needed an infusion of imagination and the encouragement to utilize that mode of thinking in order to see the world as it not only is...but especially how it *could* be."

"When I came the first night to listen to you weave your magic with words, I did so with the intention of simply allowing my mind to free itself for even a short period of time from the demands which the world has put upon me," he explained. "And yet when I heard you carry your audience away to worlds which exist only in what must be a magical realm, I found myself enthusiastically following right along while hanging on your every word. The second night of your stories, I attended with one goal in mind: to prove to myself how the illusions which you bring to life with naught but your words were simple aberrations, and as such could not possibly be sustained beyond one night."

"I am very glad to admit how I was wrong," he told me. I could feel my head swelling with every word of his praise until I feared it would burst. This was no country bumpkin offering these words; this was a learned man, a *sophisticated* man whom I had introduced to worlds beyond even *his* comprehension through a little imagination, some voice inflection, and what appeared to be a natural talent to speak.

Oh, I was loving this so!

"This is why I invited you to share supper with us last night," he explained further. "Having done the best I could to get The Duchess to experience the magic of being transported beyond reality in such a manner and failing miserably in the attempt, I wanted her to see that of which I spoke and decide for herself if indeed you could be the man we were searching for to teach our boys."

Turning to The Duchess, I just had to ask. "And was I able to get you to share in the 'magic' of which your husband refers? Do you believe I could assist in the teaching of your sons, My Lady?"

Her answer was too mumbled and too quiet to understand.

"I'm sorry My Lady, but could you possibly repeat that just a bit louder? I could not comprehend the message," I said while relishing the moment.

"This I get from Mister 'I can hear everything'?" she grumbled. I sensed reluctance from her to say that which she must. "I said that I burnt through three candles last night on my bedside table to keep away the dark!" she finally blurted out somewhat embarrassed.

Would you believe that I remained silent and said nothing? As unbelievable as it sounds, here was the easiest "checkmate" I had ever experienced being handed to me on the proverbial silver platter, and I refused to take the Queen and end the game before it had even begun.

"We spoke with the boys this morning while you slept and they both agree they would be eager to begin lessons this evening. That is, if you would favor us with another tale after dinner?" The Duke asked.

Indicating how I would be pleased to do so, I felt compelled to bring up a subject I had to admit I was reluctant to broach. "Sir...My Lady; in the short time I have known you, you have been very kind to me. It is for this reason that I feel the need to inform you that, other than acting like one upon occasion, in reality I have very little experience with children of any age. As a teacher, I fear that I may be naught but a disappointment to you in this area."

"Mister Ainsley, you appear to be an intelligent man. I am certain you could figure out how to be successful," The Duke offered.

"You would have other duties of course," The Duchess interjected, having regained her composure. "You would become one of our Staff with the same freedoms as well as responsibilities to help out, as required, to serve the people of Arlington Green."

For a-Teller-of-Tales to admit he was speechless was like saying that the sun has forgotten how to shine. Yet that was where I was none-the-less. Taking my cue from my old master The Artist, I attempted to break down all of the information I had heard plus my thoughts and my feelings into one brushstroke at a time. I discovered there were still some questions to be answered.

"You said earlier that I have a certain irreverence about me," I mentioned to The Duke. "While I would attempt to keep that fire from blazing out of control, I am who I am none the less. Would this be someone you would want interacting with your sons?"

"We would be hiring you, not some pale shadow of the man sitting before us this day. While I have absolutely *no* doubt that you will tread less than lightly upon occasion, should I find your behavior difficult, I am certain that my wife would be more than eager to help straighten you out," he said with the hint of a grin.

The Duchess now, she said not a word; she just sat there smiling, while doing her best to appear angelic.

It frankly terrified me!

"What say you Dylan?" The Duke asked finally. "Are the promises of the road—the hunger, the thirst, having tired aching feet every night, not to mention *the wolves*—offset by the feel of a soft warm bed, a roof over your head through the fiercest of storms, the knowledge of how you will never go hungry while having enough money—if spent wisely—to fill *both* of your socks? Does the lure of the wandering life hold less appeal?"

I did not give him my answer. I found that I could not. Rather, I turned to face The Duchess.

"Do you play the white king or the black king?" was all that I asked.

Reaching at Teaching

Oh, I must be in Heaven' I think to myself as I lay in my most soft and comfy bed.

It has been over four weeks since I took up residence in The Manor at Arlington Green with The Duke, The Duchess, and their boys plus the other Staff Members. I still don't think that Sir Preston trusts me fully yet, but he *has* taken to wearing his sword less often. This is good a thing, as it makes him less dangerous with both the long-pointed end as well as lessens the means for him tripping and breaking something!

My time spent with the boys is very informal; it would be hard for an outsider to discern that they are really being schooled at all. Often, we go down to the river with fishing poles in our hands and just talk about whatever is on our minds. I had them write down a host of different subjects which they were interested in hearing of or learning about and placed them in a large clay pot; Tre would pick one from the jar on Tuesdays and we would learn about that subject while Thursday is Brandon's turn to pick.

Occasionally, I would take both boys with me down to the village towards dusk when I knew a crowd would be forming looking for *something* to do for the evening. It was then I would put on my old floppy "Teller-of-Tales Hat" indicating that a tale was about to commence. I would let the boys listen to how I told the tale, what inflections in tone I utilized in order to get my points across with more emphasis and clarity, and how I reacted to comments from the audience when I listened to their questions, thoughts, and ideas. I suppose, in a way, I am teaching the entire village instead of just the boys.

Hey, maybe I should ask The Duke for a raise in my salary! I sure could use it thanks to some bone-headed moves on my part. Not only are my pockets usually empty, but my socks haven't seen a coin in weeks.

And I assure you, it's not just because of the holes in them.

And yet I do not take any of the money I am given by the grateful villagers for my efforts. Instead, I acquire the name of a family in need from one of the Village Elders prior to the performance. Early the next morning, when the family rises to begin yet another long day of hard work out in the fields or whatever may be their endeavors, they find sitting outside of their front door the proceeds of the night before wrapped up in a bright red handkerchief. The boys and I take turns sneaking up to the doors and placing the money to be found the next day; the smiles which this brings to our faces are priceless—another lesson the boys are learning without being taught from behind a desk, as it were.

As we make our way back up to The Manor and bed, we talk about the story they heard that night. Tre finally has gotten over his inevitable initial comment of "Well, it wasn't really very good but…" to honestly offering his observations or asking questions either about the tale or my manner in the telling. All of this is meant to simply get them *thinking*, not just learning. Lessons can be easy to learn, especially if they are some of the hard ones which life throws at you when you are young. But thinking of how to *handle* them—now that is another story altogether.

Sometimes I throw in tales with subjects involving points which they will undoubtedly have to deal with as they grow into responsibilities required of Nobility. I do not hide anything from them and bring up the good as well as what could be the bad side of how some Earls and Dukes treat those whose lives hang in the balance of some young Gentleman's whims. It is often when we talk about these type of topics that I can count on a visit the very next day from The Duchess to express her concerns regarding my choice of subject matter. For a response, I simply inquire if she would like me to limit my discussions to tales of fluffy little bunny rabbits, as I am certain the boys would gain so *much* knowledge from so deep a subject. Occasionally, I let her think that she has won: other times I win, and life goes on.

I really do treasure the looks which she gives me when I bring up the bunny thing!

Once I got the layout of The Manor down and became familiar with my expected scheduled responsibilities, life became quite livable. Chef handles everything for the kitchen, encompassing buying supplies, preparing and serving the meals, as well as cleaning up afterwards. I do help him with the cleaning up upon occasion—like when I am being punished for having been caught doing something not too smart and incur the wrath of either The Duke or Duchess.

Apparently, the newness of my position has worn off as I find myself spending quite a bit more time in the kitchen or helping Bryce in the stables than ever before.

When he doesn't have me to help him, Bryce handles the responsibilities of the stables including cleaning, caring and feeding the horses, and keeping the family carriage shining like new by himself. His is the deciding word on how much fodder will be required to provide hay, oats, and straw during the year, and especially how much to bring in before the winter snows so as to provide his charges with food for months at a time. Anytime there is a need for the carriage, it is Bryce who can be found driving. If a horse needs saddling it is Bryce to sees that it is done properly.

I still have yet to figure out just what it is that Sir Preston does.

While Nanny Kay's position is stated to be basically a caretaker for the boys, they have outgrown the need for such overseeing and in reality, she is much more than that. It has been many a year since she has not called The Manor home, and I suspect she will be here all the days of her life as she is so beloved by all members of the family and the Staff. She has become the Housekeeper as well as The Duchess's personal assistant, but her most critical purpose is to be the semi-official "Finder of Dylan Whenever The Duchess Requires Him." This responsibility alone can be nearly a full-time job, as one can imagine.

For in addition to my responsibilities with the boy's education, I am looked upon to handle all of the other jobs needing to be accomplished inside The Manor, outside of The Manor, or anywhere near the blasted Manor! I serve as messenger for The Duke, plus make certain that enough firewood is provided for (a responsibility which I take very seriously, as I desire to be neither cold nor hungry in the dark). Should there be any entertaining done by The Duke and Duchess, then I become not only the after-dinner entertainment, but also the one expected to handle any decorating before the event as well as the cleaning up afterwards. With all of these many jobs expected to be done by Yours Truly, you would think I never get any time to myself—and you probably would be correct—except…I did say *expected* to be done by Yours Truly! I have gotten rather adept at knowing some very good hiding places around The Manor, and when I *know* there will be some task needing to be accomplished above the norm, I have an escape route already in place which always seems to lead down to my favorite fishing spot along the river.

Perhaps now it could be understood how I find myself helping Chef or Bryce so often these days?

I do get one day a week to myself where I am not expected to meet any responsibilities unless some unforeseen monumental calamity has just taken place requiring my personal assistance in rectifying. I know this to be true as I have been here for four weeks now and, surprisingly enough, The

Duchess has found four such calamities all occurring strangely enough on the days when I am supposed to have personal time.

I must say that The Duke is very consistent in his expert handling of my complaints when I bring them to his attention. He stops whatever important matter which he has been attending to, listens to my words carefully, after which he proceeds to ask if it is true how I have received kitchen or stable duty four times that week (upon average). Being forced to answer in the affirmative, I always receive the exact same response—if one could call just staring at me without saying a word until I leave him alone a response.

I tell myself that I must be doing something right as I am still a member of The Staff. This week I may not be a *paid* member of The Staff, as I owe for the accidental breaking of a number of dishes during their washing, plus the damage done to the stables when I foolishly decided that fire would be a good way to deal with a rat I saw run under the straw of stall number two, but this week a member of The Staff I remain none-the-less.

Of course, this week isn't over yet, either!

I suppose that it is this same philosophical attitude with which I drove The Artist crazy, resulting upon my decision to try my lot as a wandering Teller-of-Tales. It is not that I do my best to destroy the plans and expectations of others, and certainly with no conceivable malice or forethought I assure you. Well, the true statement would declare at least without any *malice*. I may have many flaws. but lying is not one of them; if it were, I am certain I could have gotten out of half of my punishments over the past four weeks. What an odd situation if one contemplates it long enough: a Teller-of-Tales which are created from the fertile mind of a man who uses words to tell stories of things which are not true, and yet I do not lie!

I really do live a fascinating life.

I suppose that eventually I shall amend my ways and become more—I believe that *mature* is the word which The Duchess loves to bandy about. Heaven knows just what means it will take to make such a miracle occur.

THE ROAD TO NOWHERE LEADS EVERYWHERE

When you are traveling upon the road by yourself, it is easy to be the master of your existence. One does not stop to consider if their behavior is proper or not, as there is nobody to judge your actions but yourself. Quite frankly, I suspect that one of the major attractions of such a life was the lack of any outside influences upon my actions or my attitudes. I never stopped to consider how my behavior was being accepted, for there was never anyone else whose opinions mattered.

But now, it seems that every action I take or any word I speak is being weighed and measured—and I find I do not like this at all. I understand how important it is for me to fit in with the people who inhabit the Manor, and whom I have come to love and appreciate. Does this mean I must stop being myself and amend my behaviors in order to be acceptable to others? I have never given this kind of influence to anyone other than The Artist, and that was only after a series of arguments nearly lead me to leave his employ nearly ten years ago. Eventually, we reached an understanding as to the need for me to be who I am. Within time, The Duchess will see the many positive qualities I possess and come to the realization these will be beneficial not only to their sons, but the rest of the Manor's occupants as well. Still, I know I had best begin to pay *some* attention to the messages which I am being given.

I cannot help it but I just love to see the humor in almost any situation. If I could only learn how expressing that sentiment is not always in my best interests, I would be much better off. Even though I am often on The Duchess's bad side, I do believe she understands that I mean no disrespect to her or anyone else in The Manor. When we sit down to a game of chess, she is always pleasant and we enjoy each other's company—until the game begins, that is.

All of this is neither here nor there as today is finally my day to myself! Today I have no cares or concerns. I am going to drag myself out of this most marvelous bed, have lunch, then proceed to my fishing spot down on the river to take an afternoon nap with my floppy hat accompanying me to keep the sun out of my eyes. I have been looking forward to this day for weeks now.

Dressing in the clothes I had reserved for traveling upon the road, I stop at my door to the hallway and put an ear to the keyhole in an effort to hear if there are any calamities brewing which would require me to use escape plan number two. Hearing none, I leave my bedroom and make my way down to the kitchen to prepare some food to take with me. I see Chef, and he makes no attempt to stop me with any new punishments, so I *must* be in the clear.

Feeling the warm sunshine upon my face as I step outside, I can tell that there will be a freshening breeze down by the river—a perfect day for fishing and especially for the nap I have planned for later.

With a spring in my step, I am almost to the door on the outer wall of The Manor when I hear the clearing of a throat from behind me. Turning about, I see that it is Bryce who has made the noise. Waving a warm greeting to him, I explain how I am about to go fishing, when he responds with a simple shaking of his head back and forth.

Reading the look of confusion upon my face, he asks "Did The Duchess get exasperated again last night and ask you once more the question of when you planned to grow up?"

Shrugging my shoulders, I said that yes, I suppose that she did.

"And was your reply, 'Probably sometime in March' by any chance?" he inquired further.

Not liking the way this conversation was going, I hesitated to answer him until I reluctantly agreed that yes, I do believe that had indeed been my reply.

He never said a word in response to my admission, but rather just indicated with his finger how I was to come over to where he stood with a pitchfork and some gloves waiting for me in his hand.

Oh well, I suppose there is always *next* week!

Pawn Takes Queen

I often find myself pondering the question of when it all began. Were this an easy question to answer, I could be done contemplating and move onto bigger and more important things that I have no answers to.

I suppose that one could say before the end of the *second* week of close proximity between both antagonists, an unacknowledged state of war had been declared. Nothing overly belligerent or underhanded, you understand—just a simple case of "win at any cost" and "take no prisoners"! Sometime *between* the first and second week, a serious escalation had taken matters well beyond the tipping point. Neither side was capable of backing down and granting the other any easy victories. Although the initial movements of an aggressive nature had not been made until the third evening of week one, both parties involved had already been sizing up the other in order to determine hidden strengths and especially weakness to be exploited when the time was right.

But the first day—the very first day? While there may have been an undercurrent of challenge remaining unspoken within the first twenty-four hours, beyond that point it was undeniable how the competitive nature of both sides was one of their strongest attributes. After the first moments of their initial skirmish, it was obvious that, for either side, there was no turning back.

Perhaps the intervention of a power greater than theirs could have laid the groundwork for a peaceful solution, yet there was no mediator to be found. Quite frankly, The Duke was enjoying observing the battles, and while he never would let things get *too* far out-of-hand, the interplay certainly made for some lively evenings.

I am, of course, referring to the chess matches played after dinner was over between The Duchess and myself. We had tried to play prior to the meal, but the competitive nature of the both of us carried over to the dinner table until The Duke did intervene and declare that if we could not behave ourselves, he would burn every chessboard to be found in Arlington Green!

Don't misunderstand me: Both The Duchess and I greatly respect each other, and generally are cordial and capable of pleasant conversations... *until* we sit down to play, at which time a strange transformation takes place. Calm and cordial is replaced by the competitive nature we both share, which demands we have to overcome any challenge to come our way. Whether it be on the chessboard or in everyday life, it made no difference. While we recognize the talents and abilities of the other, we both play to win.

She is a Duchess, while I am a mere Teller-of-Tales, and yet when the match begins, we play to no social station. Regardless of her position as a member of the nobility, I neither gave nor expected any advantages nor disadvantages. I believe she appreciated that.

Or did until I began to win more often than I lost, at which time it became very obvious how this prim and proper lady could hold her own in a shouting match with a drunken sailor in some seedy dock-side bar.

For obvious reasons, the boys *must* be in bed before the game can begin.

Tonight's match holds extra importance to us both, for a wager has been made. Should The Duchess win, I am to be at her beck and call for an entire day. Should I prove to be victorious, I receive an extra day off free of any duties or responsibilities.

As has become my habit, I arrive early before The Duchess has taken her seat. I have made this the norm since the night when I discovered that honey had mysteriously been smeared upon the pieces I was to use that night. Whether this dastardly deed was initiated in response to some unknown individual placing glue on the bottom of her King the night before shall not be commented upon at this time.

Apparently, word had circulated amongst The Staff of the importance of this evening's play, for as The Duchess entered the room, she was followed by the entire household coming to enjoy what to them promised to be a most-interesting evening. Additional candles were provided courtesy of Nanny Kaye, while The Duke poured a fine wine for our enjoyment. It was when I overheard Bryce softly speaking to Chef about placing a side-bet that I knew I had better be at the top of my game. Should The Duchess be victorious, Chef would collect, while Bryce had been forced to give odds of a sort. For him to win the wager, The Duchess would have to use no less than 24 of those "special" words generally reserved for my success.

Taking her seat, we exchanged the traditional insincere wishes of good luck to the other—and the game was on!

Foregoing her usual opening in an attempt to control the middle of the board with her pawn, it was the Queen's Knight with which she made her first move. I glanced up from the board to see a smug smile upon her face, as if she were expecting some confusion upon my part due to her change of tactics. Nodding my head slightly, I did not comment upon the unusual move on her part.

Moving my gaze back to the board, I casually asked, "My Lady, do you know why the only piece which can open the game besides a pawn is the Knight?" Caught by surprise at my question, though she maintained her air of superiority, she eventually replied, "I believe it is due to being capable of jumping the pawn, Mr. Ainsley."

Placing my hand upon the piece she assumed I would use for my opening move, I turned my attention away from the board to once again gaze upon her face. While changing to another piece entirely to make my play, I answered matter-of-factly, "Actually, that move is allowed by the rules, My Lady. I should have thought you would have been aware of what those were—my mistake."

Ever wonder what a smug expression looks like when it virtually melts off someone's face? Play chess with me sometime and find out.

It was with great personal satisfaction that I overheard Bryce inform Chef, "There's three of them...twenty-one to go."

I could tell that I had shaken her confidence as her subsequent moves took longer than usual as if she was studying the board with an intensity guaranteeing her victory. Our next moves to gain position on the board involved swapping pawns for pawns, until the very moment I had picked up her fourth pawn, when she struck with blinding speed.

I could hear some of her previous swagger re-enter her voice as she inquired, "How does it feel to lose your Bishop, Mr. Ainsley?" When I countered by removing her Castle from the board with *my* move, Bryce was nearly halfway to collecting his wager.

Studying the board intently to discover the path to her mistake, she took an inordinately long period of time between moves. Initiating a casual conversation so I would not claim too much time had been taken, The Duchess made a rather remarkable observation.

"You are a very interesting fellow, Mr. Ainsley," she commented while never taking her eyes off of the board.

"I thank you for your kind words, My Lady. I must say, I do wonder in what manner they are meant?"

"In the short amount of time that you have been with us, you exhibit tendencies indicating a simple man intent upon laughter and dare I say *foolishness* in your every-day demeanor." Reaching for the piece she intended to play, she quickly withdrew he hand as if to study her strategy further. "Yet, when you sit across from me at this chessboard, I see a man of intelligence and determination as my opponent. It almost makes me wonder which of these two opposite entities is the real you."

"The answer is quite simple, My Lady," I replied. "In reality, I am both. My love of life's laughter and the enjoyment it can bring to the spirit is a large part of me—this I do freely admit. Many of my stories are indications of that particular aspect of my personality," I replied as I sipped upon my wine. "Those very same tales are also—to me at least—indications of a fertile and active mind."

Finally making her move, she looked up from the board to continue our conversation.

"I see the intelligence you possess in your interactions with Tre and Brandon—an opinion shared by both boys, I may add. For this you are to be commended," she told me while giving me the slightest of head nods as a gesture of acknowledgment. "Many of your conversations, especially around the dinner table, contain interesting points of view as well as well-thought-out topics for discussion," she added. "And yet (why does there always have to be an "and yet" after something good has been said about me?) time after time you display actions and attitudes expected of our sons, not those of a grown man. Should you ever decide to conduct yourself in a more, shall we say *grown-up* manner, I do believe that you would prove to be highly successful and, dare I say, formidable."

My attention to the game distracted and my concentration broken—her prime intention by the initiation of the conversation I am sure—I made the move I had been contemplating without thought of future ramifications to this action. Mentally disturbed by how easily she had affected my game, I attempted to swing the conversation back to where *her* level of concentration could be affected.

"Would My Lady care to offer some examples of this behavior of mine needing to be addressed?" I queried, knowing that she would need to concentrate upon her answer and not upon the game. I also had the advantage of being naturally capable of blocking-out criticism and focusing on something else—in this case, regaining my advantage.

Games within games—within games.

Unfortunately, I was too late with my intentions, as The Duchess had already plotted her strategy for the next several moves and in the process took dominant command of the game...as well as my second Bishop and both Knights!

Her swagger returning due to her changing fortunes, her voice reflected this new-found confidence.

"Oh, where to begin?" she pondered. "For there are so *many* instances to draw from."

This statement produced a muffled snickering from the assembled observers. Okay, Bryce—I *will* get even.

For the next several minutes, The Duchess produced incident after incident—at least I suspect that she did, as I was paying no attention to what she was saying. Spying an interesting opportunity on the board, I plotted my next several moves. Making the opening movement to initiate my strategy, I refocused upon her speaking to me just in time to realize she had just asked me a question. "And what was your answer to me just this morning when I asked you when you planned on growing up?"

"Was this after I had tied Chef's boot laces together as he napped in the kitchen?"

"Yes, Mister Ainsley, that would be the incident," she replied as she went back to studying the board.

"I believe my response was, *"When I get older?"*

"Exactly!" she exclaimed, her excitement heightened by the opening I had left her, which she saw as the means to my ultimate defeat.

Knowing my next moves in advance, when I saw her position her piece where I had hoped, I decided to turn the tables back upon her in an effort to distract *her* for the next two moves.

"My Lady," I began, "I do beg your indulgences for my many indiscretions. I realize how your frustrations at my behavior can be justified. I just hope that you realize how there is no malice intended." Having made this statement, I actually rose from my chair and bowed—an action which did not go unnoticed by The Duchess. Feeling well pleased at seeing the look of surprise upon her face, I realized that I had accomplished my objective and completely destroyed her concentration.

Not wishing to relinquish this advantage, I proceeded to further extend my remarks.

"While it may be considered a flaw in my character, thanks to the generous offer you and your husband bestowed upon me when you welcomed me into your home, for the first time in quite a while I now have a tendency to look upon life as an experience to be enjoyed." In reality, what I was stating was the truth. While my message was heart-felt—and one I freely wished to convey, can I help it if my timing may not have been the best?

"Have I gotten carried away by opportunities to express this new-found attitude?" I knew my inquiry would require her to answer, and thus keep her attention from my countering move.

"While I can appreciate the improvement of your view upon life, I must concur that your zeal needs to be tempered by *some* degree of restraint." I could not help but notice her eyes widen by what she saw upon the board.

Needing to keep her attention elsewhere so as not to discover the trap I was preparing, I continued to express some opinions which I had never previously.

"My Lady, I must tell you that you—and your husband as well, of course—are truly marvels to me." Now *that* got her attention. "The few experiences I have ever had involving members of the nobility have been of a different nature completely. I have been met by arrogance, airs of superiority, as well as a complete lack of respect." I continued talking, doing my best to keep the excitement I was feeling from my speech when I saw her reaching for her Queen. "Yet the both of *you* have been naught but kind to me. This was certainly not an attitude I was expecting when I was first invited to spend an evening with you and share a tale or two. I just want you to know that you have my deepest respect." Watching her move her Queen into position to bring about my anticipated downfall, I included, "as well as my love."

Catching her by surprise with my last statement, she felt the need to turn her attention to me as she replied with appreciation to my kind words.

"I assure you that they are heart-felt and genuine," I smiled as I proceeded with my next move.

As she began to study the board once again, I needed to make sure she did not see the danger I had put her in—thus I continued my gambit.

"I just wish the both of you to know that not only do I respect your position in life, I fully appreciate the people you have proven yourselves to be. The trust you have placed in me with the tutoring of your sons I draw confidence in...especially as I have had so little interaction with young people prior to this opportunity. I will refrain from any more speech," I told her innocently, "for I do not wish tears to fall upon so magnificent a chessboard."

As if without thinking, she brought her Castle into play, assuring her victory with her next move—and sealing her doom.

Reaching out to place my fingers upon what could be considered the most insignificant piece upon a chessboard, I moved a lowly pawn forward. Pausing for a moment to allow her the opportunity to see the consequences of ignoring what I had orchestrated, it was with great personal satisfaction when I announced "Checkmate!"

Within the next several moments I heard the clapping of hands, I experienced the look of amazement upon the face of The Duchess, and I knew that Bryce had won his bet with Chef!

Rising from my seat as she got up to leave, I offered to The Duchess congratulations upon a game well played. Her mumbled reply of the same to me indicated her true opinion of the match. Pausing only to whisper into The Duke's ear, she rapidly departed the room without another word spoken.

"Well, My Boy, that certainly was an interesting game—on many levels," The Duke observed as he came over to where I was standing. "Congratulations upon a well-deserved victory," he said as he offered me his hand.

"Thank you, Sir," I replied as I shook that hand. "I just want you to know that I meant every word of what I said during the game. I would appreciate it if you could pass this along to The Duchess, as I suspect she does not wish to speak with me at this moment."

"I shall be glad to do so," he assured me with a smile. "Once she calms down, of course. And I do believe your assessment to be accurate, as she wished me to pass along to you the answer to your inevitable question of when you can expect to receive the free day you have won."

Rubbing my hands together in anticipation of enjoying a day of fishing and extended napping, I could barely hide my excitement as I asked, "And just when would that day be, Sir?"

Unable to hide a grin of his own, The Duke replied, "I believe the words that she used were "When you get older," or something to that effect."

Checkmate!

Lessons Learned from a Desk

From my position as Teller-of-Tales of the Manor, it honestly has been enjoyable for me to watch The Duke and Duchess's two sons grow up. I believe I am enjoying it so much because I am personally assisting them to do so. I am taking notes on the ways which The Duke and Duchess teach their children—you know, just in case I ever should have any of my own someday.

I greatly admire how they are training their boys to be "Noble Nobility." By this, I mean that in spite of the fact that Tre and Brandon are born into the Upper Class, they are being taught how all people are *people* regardless of their station in life. Everyone deserves respect. Yes, even Tellers-of-Tales, thank you very much.

The Duke believes in checks and balances: power demands responsibility, rights demand respect, and when it's needed, a right demands a left! I have heard him say in the past that in reality, a Ruler is a servant...the pay's just better. A proper Ruler that is, not a petty tyrant who gets rich on the backs of others. He says that as a Duke, you have to C.A.R.E., which stands for Communicate, Appreciate, Respect, and something that begins with "E" that I can *never* remember.

It's a lesson which the boys have accepted well, although there are times when the natural urge to make everyone know you are someone special gets the better of them.

The incident of "The Desk" was indeed one such time.

The boys had just returned home after spending time in the Capital, where The Duchess had taken them to visit with some of the other Noble families and gain a bit of an education in the ways of the Royal Court. There was a distinct air about them when they returned, for a sense of superiority was wafting about them. If I could see it, then rest assured that The Duke could as well.

The discussion around the table after dinner that evening was what to do with the extra funds that a larger than expected harvest would bring to Arlington Green. As we occasionally *do* give The Duke and Duchess some worthy ideas, the floor was opened to the rest of the Staff on what should be done with the extra revenue. Some very good ideas were forthcoming—of course one was mine—while some silly responses were mixed in as well.

The concept of giving all of the Staff members a raise was shot down immediately.

Fine, I'll just keep my mouth shut then!

Bryce observed that as parts of the stonework on the outer wall were in need of repair, perhaps some of the funds should go to address that need. The Duke responded that while he agreed with the idea, it would not be fair for us to take all of the hard-earned extra money from the villagers and use it for ourselves. Therefore, he would finance the necessary work on the walls directly from the family treasury.

It was at this point when Tre piped in with, "Why *shouldn't* we use the money for what we want? It's all ours anyway."

His outburst was met with silence, the crackling of the wood in the fireplace the only sound to be heard within the room.

The Duke turned to his oldest son and asked him to explain what he meant.

"One of the topics which we boys discussed amongst ourselves in the Capital was our homes and how regal and opulent they were," Tre answered. "Brandon and I were surprised at first to discover how most if not all of the Manors, and *especially* The Palace were adorned with large amounts of artwork, tapestries, and very lush gardens. I asked how they could afford such riches; I was told that their fathers collect very high levies from the towns which they own, keeping the people hungry and themselves well fed. In fact," he continued sounding somewhat embarrassed, "we were given more than a few strange looks as if we were from some unworthy "Minor Country Manor" or something. If their fathers are Dukes or Earls, and they have so much because they own everything, then why couldn't we just take the extra money and use it how we see fit?"

Brandon nodded his head in approval of what his brother had just said.

The flickering flames of the many candles within the dining room played upon the face of The Duke as he looked long and hard at his sons. It was the perfect time for the rest of the Staff to be done with dinner and excuse themselves…fast.

One by one, we rose to leave as we knew a "heart-warming" lecture was about to take place. Nanny Kaye was closest to the door, so she made it out first, followed closely by Bryce, Sir Preston, and then Chef. I was just reaching the door when I heard "Dylan, stay a minute, would you?"

"Sit down please," The Duke asked me, indicating my usual place at the table whose occupants now consisted of only The Duke and Duchess, their two sons, and me—just a *happy* little family gathering.

The Duke stared long and hard at his sons; neither was able to withstand that gaze very long. I could see that The Duchess was squirming in her seat, as if her idea of taking the boys to the Capital would now be looked upon as pretentious and conflicting. A look was exchanged between The Duke and his wife. Yep, it was.

If she was squirming, it was nothing in comparison to the butt dances the boys were performing in *their* chairs at the moment. Knowing their father pretty well, they anticipated a very long stern lecture at best, while at the worst...well, at least good-old Dylan is here to document their demise in tale and song!

Why *was* good-old Dylan here? Naturally, my first reaction was, 'What did I do wrong?' due to well-earned experiences many times in the past. My second reaction was to join the rest of the dance team with squirming in my chair, as I had yet to hear how I was in the clear.

Folding his hands together to rest upon the table, The Duke informed his sons that he had a task for them to complete and would like Dylan to oversee their efforts, if I would be so kind.

Kind? Hey, kind is my middle name—as long as I was in the clear of course. I nodded approval, not yet knowing what I had just signed up for.

"In the next three days," he continued, beginning to outline their project, "each of you boys will create a wooden desk to the best of your ability. There will only be two rules involved in its completion, but these both *must* be obeyed to the letter! Do you boys understand?"

Emphatic nodding of their heads indicated either they understood, or that they weren't going to take any chances of disturbing their father any further. Me—I had no clue, so I just sat there without moving as I did not want to have to create a full kitchen table with chairs.

"The two rules to be followed are these: first, you can only use items which you will find in the woods and fields to create this desk, and secondly you will work on them for a minimum of twelve hours per day. If they are not completed on time, you will be *severely* punished. Do you understand?" he asked both of his sons.

It was difficult to tell if they truly did know what he expected, yet they indicated acceptance none-the-less.

I glanced over at The Duchess. Her face certainly indicated concern for what she had just heard. It was only the trust which years of experience in The Duke had given her that kept her nervous anticipation silent.

Smiling inwardly at what he perceived as their dilemma, The Duke continued with more instruction. "Dylan will be available for *supervision*, but he is not allowed to assist you with any construction of your desks. You have three days…no more! You are excused," he dismissed them, kissing each in turn as they quickly left the room for bed.

As the boys took their leave, I could tell from the expressions on their faces that a long, restful sleep was not to be had *this* night.

Taking this as my cue to leave as well, I almost made it to the door once again when I was asked to remain behind, after which The Duke explained his motives.

"So, you understand what I am about then?" he asked me once he had outlined his intentions.

"Yes Sir, I do indeed," I assured him. "We shall see just what is produced in three days' time." I got out of there as quickly as I could, as The Duke now turned his full attention upon The Duchess.

The hour was late when I eventually climbed into my own bed, my preparations for the coming day finally completed.

I roused the boys at sunup, several hours before they would normally be getting out of bed. Two heavily yawning boys found dirty and more than slightly *aromatic* work clothes ready and waiting for them. A breakfast, consisting of a very thin soup of mostly water which I had arranged with Chef the prior evening, was given to them as they dressed.

Indicating displeasure at the smell of the clothes he was to wear, Tre wondered where the toast and hot tea were.

"They're up in the Manor being eaten by an Earl's Son and not meant for a common laborer," I answered him abruptly. "Besides, your time for eating has passed." I indicated the door. "It's to the outside world for you—get to work!"

Tre looked at me as if I had just grown horns and a barbed tail. "Why are you behaving this way?" he asked, knowing full well that this was not my normal demeanor.

"I am not the Dylan whom you know," I explained. "I am, in reality, an Overseer instructed by my protector, The Duke of Wayne, to get the most work out of his laborers as can be done. You're already late so stop stalling and get a move on!"

Stepping out into the gloomy hallway of a Manor House full of still-sleeping inhabitants, I took the opportunity to explain their tasks further. "Each of you boys will be given a simple axe, plane, and knife to use for your efforts. Because you will work in the same area, I suggest that you work as quickly as you can, for the available resources can become very limited. Do you really want to go back and tell your father how you ran out of material while your brother has his desk completed?" I inquired while already knowing the answer.

Could it have been the effect of the sputtering torches flickering across the faces or did I only imagine their eyes doubling in size in reaction to my last question?

"And Gentlemen," I stated emphatically while stopping just inside of the front door and giving them my best stern expression, "look not to your parents for excuses, laziness, or failure." I showed them what I was holding in my hand. "I have been given orders that if I should find either of you giving less than one hundred percent effort at any time during the next three days, I am not only free to use this—I am *expected* to. I suggest that you do not tempt me."

Their eyes *definitely* became the size of saucers as they looked at the whip which I held in my hands!

Now I would never use it on those boys; *I* knew that, The Duke knew that, but *they* did not! Just in case, I had embellished the whip with a little persuader for effect.

"Dylan, what is that rust color splashed along the leather?" Tre wanted to know.

I gave him my best "I'm a rotten bugger" look and said simply, "Blood… want to add to it?" I had actually taken some wine and splashed it over the leather last night, but strangely enough I forgot to tell them that little truth.

It was actually a cold morning as the sun had yet to make a difference in the day. "Dylan, where are our jackets?" Brandon wondered as he stepped out of the warm house and into the chill.

"You have none," I answered him simply. "The money which could have bought you some warmth was used by The Earl to buy his daughter some new dress for an upcoming party. Just be hopeful that the sun warms you soon."

I was almost beginning to get scared; I was really *good* at playing this part.

Picking up their tools and gaining some small cuts in the process, we made our way out to the edge of the eastern woods.

"Start collecting your materials," I told them as I sat down under a comfortable tree and dropped my hat over my eyes. "First one who makes me get up gets no lunch, and the second one gets the same. You are dependent on each other for any reward or punishment which is forthcoming."

Settling into the notch of my tree, I watched the efforts of the boys from under the rim of my hat. They are no strangers to work; their father has made sure of that, but not work to this level and magnitude. It was only a matter of time until backs would become sore, arms tired, and throats parched.

The sun was climbing into the morning sky when Tre asked if they could take a break.

"Are you finished with your project?" I casually inquired, taking a drink from my flask.

"No," was his answer.

"Then no," was *my* answer. "Get back to work!"

Noon time came around, and the boys had acquired quite a number of larger pieces of wood, some small branches for the making of knobs for the drawers, and Tre had even found a few pieces of flint.

I was curious and asked about the flint.

"I want to give my desk a shade of darker brown, so if I light a small fire and hold the wood over the fire, I can blacken parts as I desire," he explained. "I want to make this the best darn desk my father has ever seen."

That was an outstanding idea: good thought processes coupled with top notch reckoning. It *must* be the result of my influence.

"So, what is for lunch? I'm starved," Brandon added to the conversation.

"How does fresh bread, pieces of warm ham, apples, and cool tea sound?" I asked cheerfully as I rose from my seat as if to be ready to go get lunch.

I must have hit the right spot as huge smiles grew on both of their faces

"Sounds perfect to me," announced Tre with his mouth watering, his reaction echoed emphatically by his younger brother.

"Good," I said while settling back into the comfort of my spot on the ground. "Because that's exactly what they are having up in the Manor just now. *You* on the other hand get to eat your hunger and drink your own sweat. Bon appetite."

"Dylan, why are you being this way?" Tre asked, for he knew that this was not my true nature. My answer did little to ease his concern.

"Boy, you need to get into your head that for the next three days, I am *not* the Dylan you know. I am an Overseer of field hands—that would be you two. You, on the other hand, are not sons of The Duke of Arlington Green, but are run-of-the-mill village boys. No more, no less." Once again

I rose to stand, my finger jabbing into each of their chests for effect. "You will work as they do, eat as they eat, and be treated as they are. When they eat, you eat. When they drink, you drink. Understand?"

"Wait a minute—" Tre started, only to be startled back by the crack of my whip.

I quickly turned my hand away so he wouldn't see the trickle of blood where the recoil had taken a slice out of my flesh. I never have been very good with a whip.

"Do you think this is how you talk to me, you village swine?" I angrily demanded as I approached the two frightened boys threateningly. "Your rest is now over. Get back to work or you will feel my next lash upon your backs!"

Picking up his tools with a bit of a tremble in his hands, Tre timidly asked, "Sir, may I ask a question?"

"As you have discovered manners, you may ask," I retorted, flicking the whip once again.

My hand really did hurt!

"I have watched our village workers in the fields many times, and they are not treated anywhere in this manner," he observed rightfully. "Why are we being subjected to this?"

"You forget: you are not freemen from the village of Arlington Green," I explained with a sneer. "You two are lowly serfs of The Duke of Wayne who cares nothing for his people. All he wants is profits so he can live as regally as he can. And why not?" I questioned nastily. "He owns *everything* after all. He even owns *you!*"

I pointed slowly at both of them again for added emphasis. "Cattle have as many rights as you do here. Now no more questions; get your butts back to work!"

The scowl never left my face as I settled back into my comfortable tree. Wishing I had an audience observing my performance other than the two boys who certainly could not appreciate how well I was playing this part, I inwardly smiled at my efforts.

The afternoon went pretty much the same as had the morning, possibly without as many surprises for the boys. The toll on their bodies became more noticeable, for with the passing of each and every hour, they were moving slower and slower. As long as they kept going I kept quiet and mentioned it not.

As the sun was going down, I signaled how work was done for the day. "Bring your tools with you and we will return in the morning to start carrying what you have prepared to where you can begin shaping the wood. Step lively now, for I am hungry," I ordered.

The trip back to the Manor was one of the quietest times I ever experienced on stage or off. These boys were dog tired. It was Tre who eventually broke the silence. "A quick dinner for me and right into my nice soft bed," he mentioned to Brandon, who was in exactly the same mindset.

I let those daydreams last for all of a few seconds, then dashed them up against another wall. "Beds, dinner—those are for the Nobility at the Manor," I reminded them. "You are field hands, remember? A light supper, then you may have your sleep—in the stables. That is, after you get your chores done of course."

"*The stables!*" Tre blurted. "Why in heaven's name are we to sleep with the animals?"

"Why not?" I answered his question with one of my own. "In winter time, peasants have to provide warmth for their animals or they would freeze. If all you have is a one-room house, as many of these families do, with no attached shed or barn, the only way to keep their sheep, cows, or pigs alive is to bring them inside with them and their families. Just imagine," I said thoughtfully "how wonderful your day would begin if, as you get out of your warm bed in the morning, you proceed to step in a big steaming pile of poop dropped by one of your pigs during the night. Pretty good life, don't you think?" I was not expecting to get an answer.

You could see their backs bend lower than the bottom of a caterpillar's feet. Their faces reflected total disbelief. This had to be a bad dream!

If they were hurting today, just wait until they woke up in the morning with stiff muscles. I truly was feeling sorry for them, but more importantly, I understood the message which The Duke was going to impart into his sons. Three days of their pain certainly beats a lifetime of pain for many others.

They stored their tools in the stable entrance, after which they eagerly wolfed down a small sandwich and some weak tea that Chef had left just for them.

"Here is where I must bid you adieu," I told them. "I have a fine dinner waiting for me, as well as a nice soft bed. Good thing too—I'm *so* tired!" I lied while stretching for effect. "Your 'Uncle' will take over from here. See you in the morning bright and early."

I passed out of the stable, leaving two young boys whose chins had just dropped down to their knees.

I passed Bryce standing in the shadows. "They're all yours, My Friend," I whispered. "I'll be back in the morning to gather up what's left."

Doing his best to produce a scowl, Bryce walked into the light of the stable. "Good evening boys," he said, clapping his hands together. "Now, which side of the stables are we to clean before bedtime?"

I hurried to the Dining Room as dinner was about to begin. In between bites I gave The Duke detailed descriptions of the day's events and interactions. The Duchess was nervous and apprehensive for their boys, but The Duke was very pleased. He gave me some new thoughts for tomorrow's efforts.

It was The Duchess who spoke to me last as I was leaving for the evening. "Dylan, please remember: the boys are to hurt, not to *be* hurt."

I gave her a look of honest disbelief. "My Lady," I told her, "I would no more hurt those two boys than if they were my own sons. That is why I play the charade I do. They will be *sore*, and they will be *sorry*, but they will not be marred in any way. That is my vow to you—and to them. I take no pleasure in that act nor in the pain that I am inflicting on your sons."

In no way did I enjoy tormenting the boys! The Duke had ordered it, the boys had accepted it, and I was going to see it through regardless of what I was feeling. In a strange way, both The Duke and his sons would benefit from this action. I just got to hate myself for making it happen.

I sought out Chef as he cleared the table and explained what I would like him to do the next day. As usual, he was more than willing to oblige.

Once again, I was up before the crack of dawn. Thank goodness this charade was only for three days—this early rising effort was getting to be a very bad habit.

Entering the stables with the light breakfast which I had once again procured from Chef, I found both boys fast asleep. Bryce informed me how they had worked almost until midnight completing their task.

I let him know what a good job he was doing. "Tonight, let's give them a few hours after their dinner alone," I told my good friend. "I want to see what their reaction is at that point. See you this evening."

Picking up an iron drum and a ladle, I proceeded to bang on the drum not even five feet from the sleeping youths. "Rise and shine," I exclaimed. "Work is calling. You have five minutes to eat, drink, and prepare yourselves for the long day ahead."

Shock, realization turning to immediate dread. Not bad for the first five seconds of their being awake. The stiffness hit next as it easily took both of them a good two minutes just to get themselves up.

Leaving our tools behind, we traveled to the site of yesterday's work and their previously gathered materials. For the next three hours, the boys labored back and forth from the site to the Manor work area and back again. I made sure that the loads were not too heavy, but certainly not too light as the sweat on their brows indicated. They spent the rest of the day making rough boards out of their wood with the axes, planes, and knives. I kept close by and very watchful as the sharp tools they were using could really do some damage.

Once again there was no lunch.

Once again rest periods were not forthcoming.

To the accompaniment of the sounds of wood being chopped and shaped, the boys worked on throughout the day. They slowed down the later it became but towards the end of the day, the rudimentary outlines of two desks began to take shape.

At the setting of the sun, we got back to the stables where Chef was doling out their meager dinner.

"Those sure are nice knives you boys have there," he said in admiration as the tools were set aside for the night. "Nice and sharp and long. I bet those would work well for me in the kitchen." Bidding the two boys a good night, Chef told me of what a marvelous meal he had prepared for tonight's table. "Dinner will be a bit late, so there's no hurry Dylan," he informed me as he was leaving.

Pretending to take no notice of the whispering being exchanged between the boys, I happily announced "Okay boys, I am off. Bryce will be back after dinner to work the other half of the stables, I would imagine. Get some rest."

I made plenty of noise leaving the stable and while walking across the courtyard and to the side door. As soon as the door was closed, I sprinted to the closest window, which just *happened* to be open, climbed out, and joined Bryce in the darkness of the shadows as we both settled down to watch the events transpire. We talked softly about what the boy's next move would be. I bet him one silver coin (my life's savings) that within half an hour the boys would be sneaking down to the door of the kitchen. He felt they would be too tired and not go anywhere and accepted the wager.

It took all of ten minutes for me to double my life savings as the boys snuck out of the stable and down towards the back door of the kitchen. We were not close enough to hear the knock made upon the door, but within a minute, Chef answered. They stood talking for a few minutes during which two long sharp knives were displayed. Chef disappeared but returned several minutes later with two thick sandwiches and some cider that he exchanged for the knives. He played his part very well, even to the point of looking around as if to make sure no one would see him make the trade.

The two younger conspirators slipped back into the stables, where within a few minutes the sound of boyish laughter could be heard.

Bryce and I smiled to each other. He paid me my winnings, and we left the two tricksters for the comfort of the dinner table.

Giving my update of the events of the day during dinner, when I explained the cleverness of one Tre and Brandon, the table's occupants could not help but laugh. Still, The Duke was pleased at the resourcefulness which the two had shown.

It took everything I had not to shoot that dang rooster with an arrow as dawn crept into view. I got up anyway, at least knowing how this was the last day of this debacle.

Getting the boys up and ready proved to be more difficult than *my* efforts at rising. They were so sore they could hardly move. A little dunk into "Dr. Dylan's Barrel of Magical Rainwater" took care of their malady quickly.

We made our way back to our work area and set about on completing their task. Tre, being the oldest, naturally was putting more expertise into his desk. Brandon, bless his heart, tried his best to do a good job. Neither was a skilled craftsman, but you could definitely tell that these pieces of wood were what they were supposed to be. Tre had loosely set in several drawers using the fire idea to give the wood some texture and color. Brandon spent the last hour trying to fill in the many holes his effort had constructed.

In spite of all that they had endured for the past three days, I could see pride in their eyes as they took one last look at their two desks. When something is created out of adversity by your own two hands, there really are no proper words to describe the feeling one gets. But their two smiles did a pretty good job of revealing their feelings.

I got Bryce to help me carry the desks into the dining room. I told the boys to go get cleaned up before dinner, as everyone would be attending that evening to share in the celebration of their efforts.

I knew what was about to happen—that doesn't mean I had to *like* it!

When the boys returned clean enough to at least tell who they were, everyone else was seated around the table while dressed in their finest clothes, making merry when the boys entered the room as if a party was going on.

Standing by the fire, The Duke motioned the boys forward to stand before him.

"I see that you have completed the task set before you," he said while inspecting their handiwork. "Two desks, each made with care and attention are set here before me; the very pride of your work. I am impressed with your efforts," he told two very tired but very proud young boys. "But I fear it is getting a bit *cold* in here don't you think?" He turned to address us seated at the table. "I do believe that we need some extra heat in here for our illustrious guests."

He looked the uncomprehending boys directly in the eyes as he commanded, "Now each of you take your desk, break it into pieces and throw them into the fire."

Tre and Brandon were stunned.

The ladies looked away. They could not watch as the boys completed this last task. The gaiety of the evening had dissolved into an eerie uneasy silence.

"Excuse me, Father," Tre asked in disbelief. "Did you say throw them into the *fire?*"

"Yes, I did. And be quick about it!" The Duke snapped.

Slowly as if in a dream, both Tre and Brandon did their best to pick up the pride of their work, destroy the fruits of their efforts, and fling them to eminent destruction. The tears in their eyes were matched by most of the occupants of the table, I can assure you.

"Come here, boys," The Duke called to them after the deed was done.

They came to stand in front of him, the brightness of the enhanced fire clearly showing their heads bowed low, for no boy wants to have their father see them cry.

"You have just spent the past three days living the life of a serf in one of those opulent Manors which you were so impressed with," he began evenly with his hands upon their shoulders. "The days were long, and your bellies were empty. Hard work, sweat, and more than a little blood went into your effort. You had *pride,*" he told them, "and deservedly so in what you had created."

"Yet at the very moment when you had an opportunity to show *something* for your efforts, it was snatched away from you for the convenience of someone who takes what they want from whoever they wish, by the power of Divine Right," The Duke continued gravely. "Remember how it feels Lads. Never let it fail to grip your insides all of the days of your lives."

After allowing several moments for the boys to think about what he had said, The Duke went on.

"You now know how the villagers would feel if we took all of the profits which their hard work had reaped in the fields for our own means. And don't forget," he added earnestly, "you lived this life for only *three* days. There are poor souls out there who do what you did every single day of the year with no chance of *ever* escaping their lot."

He motioned the boys to come closer and find solace in his outstretched arms.

"I truly am sorry that this had to be endured, yet I feel that the message which you learned is well worth the cost." They nestled in his arms. "What have ye to say?"

There was silence for a moment or two, then it was Tre who found strength in his voice.

"I guess I never realized just how much pretty things can cost," he said while gazing up at his father. "Especially when you are dealing with real people. I let greed take over my thinking. I had forgotten the lessons which you have taught us." Hanging his head, he could say no more.

Brandon tried to get his thoughts out, yet it was more difficult for him as he was younger and had not yet experienced all of the training his older brother had. "I *like* our old Manor and never want to see those other people's places ever again," he offered.

"Yet we *too* live in a Manor and want for little," added The Duchess. "We could have all of those fineries which you so eagerly described if we wished. Sometimes, the thrill of gold makes one leave their senses in its pursuit. Remember, it's not *what* you have that matters—it's the person you *are* that is important."

I felt I needed to add a point as I was there through all of this.

"You had to make a decision last night: do you keep your knives or get some food for your empty bellies," I began.

Both boys looked startled in that their cleverness had been found out.

"Never mind about that," I told them with a wave of my hand. "But just imagine if you truly were one of those serfs whom your father speaks about. You have tools—not many or very good, but enough for you to complete your job to feed yourselves and your families. Can you imagine what heartache it would cause to have to make the decision which you did in the real world?" I asked. "By sating the immediate hunger of your children, you ensure that you will have to work even *harder*—if it is possible—just to get the same which you have always had. That could be a very hard choice indeed."

I got nodded heads from them for my comment in addition to a quietly mouthed, "Thank You," from The Duchess.

The mood around the table after this was truly a party atmosphere, for the boys were back. All congratulated them for the desks they had crafted. Smiles replaced tears as the night wore on, which were very soon replaced by drooping eyes on the faces of two very tired young boys.

Make that *three* of us.

A Festival Occasion

One evening upon dinner being completed, The Duke took the opportunity to announce that because everyone has been working diligently lately (why did all heads turn in my direction when he said that?) a short respite was in order. In three days' time, the entire household would gather early in the morning to begin a five-day journey to attend The Semi-Annual Festival of Music before returning back home again. Excited voices flew about the table as first one and then another expressed our anticipation of a wonderful experience, as well as sincere gratitude for being included. Naturally there would be many preparations to attend to, and this was one instance when I did not even attempt to shirk any efforts needed done by Yours Truly.

The Semi-Annual Festival of Music, just as its title indicates, occurs twice a year at various locations across the country. All of the best talents throughout The Realm, known artists and undiscovered ones, would be in attendance, vying for the highly coveted title of Festival Winner. Careers were made or broken depending on one's showing upon that stage. Thus, every year it seemed that the competition became fiercer as individuals, duos, trios, and entire ensembles performed—but only one would be declared the winner. The choices of the judges were not always agreed with. However, it was agreed upon that the vocal talent was the absolute very best and whoever took home the title would have their professional career made for life.

Having written a number of songs during my wanderings, I was anxious to attend and hear the work of other songwriters, regardless how inferior they proved themselves to be. Still, while our ears were to be treated to a feast, it was my belly which was really looking forward to The Festival. Row upon row of the finest cooks and bakers would also be entrenched in those fields anxious to have their wares sampled. You know me and my desire to help out—I would do my part to assure that their entries were not in vain. Fortunately for us all, Chef was going to attend with the rest of the household assuring that he would be returning home with some excellent new recipes for us all to enjoy and probably a new five pounds for himself.

Two days before we were slated to leave for The Festival, I was helping Bryce ready both family carriages for the journey when I asked him where it was to be held this season. Admitting that he did not know, I suggested that perhaps it may be a good idea if the driver of the lead carriage had at least a small glimmer of what direction we were headed—maybe even an inkling perhaps of where we would like to end up? Indicating how he had complete faith in The Duke to share such highly secretive information in good time with him and the other coach's driver Chef, I expressed agreement. Then I went to find a copy of a map of the surrounding area just in case.

Later at dinner, Bryce's faith in The Duke proved well founded. Chef was instructed to prepare lunch for the upcoming journey as it would not be until later in the evening before we would arrive at our destination of…
Brighton!

Fighting down an urge to be sick at hearing the name of the town where I had led 16 terrified children to safety from the debacle of Brackensburg, my heart stopped mid-beat at the thought of re-living that nightmare afresh by visiting the scene of its occurrence. I must have turned pale when The Duke mentioned the name, for Bryce turned to me and whispered how he had never seen me so scared and asked if I was okay. My mouth formed the words that indicated I was fine; the shaking of my hands as they gripped the arms of my chair proved otherwise. Quietly gaining the attention of The Duke, Bryce tilted his head in my direction, and the slightest returning nod indicated that the message had indeed been received.

Feigning illness for my sudden loss of appetite, I asked to be excused. To my chagrin, I found that I could barely stand until I felt the two strong hands of Bryce helping me to my feet. Insisting that he accompany me to my room, we left to looks of bewilderment being shared by those remaining seated. My eyelids clamped down tightly as if to keep the visions within my mind at bay. I trusted in Bryce's guidance as he nearly carried me down the hall. I could sense that he was speaking, but his words went unheeded as my ears were deaf to all but the echoing screams of the damned as they died by the score!

Gaining the security of my room, Bryce gently laid me down on my bed and pulled up a chair. Instinctively lighting some additional candles to overcome the shadows, his face betrayed his concern as he asked me to share what was bothering me so.

Looking into the eyes of the man I could honestly say was the best friend I have ever known, I found that no matter how hard I tried, I could not get my tongue to couple with the torment raging within my mind and offer him any explanation for my actions. Several times I came close to forming the words but the sound died on my tongue; in spite of the trust he held, I could not break free of my panic and confide in him. Rolling away from having to face him and read his disappointment and concern, I managed to offer thanks for his help. Waiting a few minutes longer in silence while hoping that I could speak with him, he eventually left me to my own devices and one very long and very *sleepless* night.

Early the next morning, I sought an audience with The Duke, during which I requested to be left behind when they departed for The Festival. I suggested how it would be prudent for one member of The Staff to remain in the event of an emergency. Indicating that The Village Elders were fully capable of handling any matters of importance until we returned five days hence, he asked me the real reason why I felt I could not attend.

Unable to look him directly in the eye, I said that my reasons were my own and asked him to allow me the courtesy of refusing to answer. Anywhere but in Arlington Green, speaking to a Noble thusly could and probably *would* result in a punishment most severe. However, I was speaking to The Duke of Arlington Green, who I had learned to trust and love.

Long he looked at me, until with a shaking of his head, he simply told me, "No." Before I could offer protest, he raised his hand to stop me in my tracks.

"Something is troubling you to an extent I have never seen before," he said, the depth of his concern evident in his voice. "All too often I have seen men haunted by events of their past until they become mere shells of their former selves. There is something about Brighton which threatens you with this happening," he declared, "and that is something which I cannot allow you to do to yourself."

"Dylan, in a very short time, you have grown to be as a member of our family. All love you and wish you happiness," he continued with a softening of his voice. "Whatever hold the ghosts of Brighton have upon you, unless faced, they shall triumph and Dylan will be lost forever. That is something which I will *not* allow," he informed me with resolve. "Together we will face them and exorcise them once and for all. No, you may *not* remain behind. Rather you will accompany us on this journey— unless you wish to run away in the dead of night. Of that I have no fear or concern, for I do not believe you to be a coward of any sort. If I did, then quite frankly we would be leaving within the hour. As it is, be prepared, for we leave at dawn."

While I would spend the rest of my life thanking him for his words, I was not ready to at this time. Nodding my head as acknowledgement of his decision, I left the room in silence.

While no more was said on the matter, I couldn't help but notice an uncomfortable atmosphere throughout the day as preparations were made for the travel the next morning. If I should happen to enter a room where a conversation was taking place, all talking would immediately cease and resume only when I had departed. One would expect dinner to be rather animated that evening, as the excitement of the next five days should be the topic for all manner of discussions. Instead, silence was served as the main course with a heaping helping of lack of conversation for desert.

Once dinner was over, I helped Bryce load the coaches as the Manor's occupants would bring down their trunks containing their clothes and such for us to stow aboard. Our task completed, we bid each other goodnight and departed for our rooms to answer the calls of our awaiting beds.

The sputtering of torches mounted in the hallways gave off splotches of light amidst the darkness as I skulked down the hall as quietly as I could later that night. Opening the door to the outer courtyard only as wide as necessary for me and the bag upon my back to squeeze outside, I made my way to the coach where earlier I had stowed my clothing for the expedition. I was just about to reach inside the storage compartment when the bright light of a lantern cut the night air to settle directly into my eyes.

"Sort of late for a stroll, isn't it Dylan?" the voice of Bryce inquired as he stepped out from the shadows to come stand beside me. Lowering the lantern in order to detect what I had been carrying, when he saw what it was, he stepped between me and the coach. He closed and *locked* the storage area, after which he doused the light while remaining by my side.

"You know...if I was the suspicious type, I would be wondering why you would be placing everything you own in the world there along with your other clothes," he said matter-of-factly.

Angry at having been caught in this manner, I asked him just what the blazes he was talking about? "Who says that this is all of my possessions in so small a bag?" I demanded.

"Dylan, trust me, I know what I am talking about," he replied in convincing fashion. "I've been to your room several times and know how little you truly own. That bag is just about the size to hold it all. Not really a very big bag is it?" he jokingly asked in an effort to make light of the tension between us.

"If you want to play at being some Master Sleuth, be my guest," I said as if to mock his efforts. "But suppose you tell me why I would be doing whatever I think that you are thinking I had thought up, for I am all ears."

Refusing to take the bait and become argumentative, he went back to his original theme. "Well now, if I *were* the suspicious type, I would surmise that you were sneaking everything you owned on the coach because you were thinking of maybe leaving us sometime during the Festival—or perhaps before we had even arrived," he mentioned in frustratingly maddening sureness of his correctness.

The trouble was, he was precisely right!

"Since when it is any business of yours just what I do?" I demanded hotly.

His words echoed his mellowed thoughts as he simply replied, "When I saw how you reacted to The Duke's announcement of our destination, I decided to *make* it my business." He paused for only a moment before he asked a question requiring no answer. "Isn't that what friends do?"

I found that I became inwardly relieved at having been stopped in my efforts, as the inner turmoil within my mind caused by panic subsided at hearing his words. Deciding right then and there that I would face whatever this excursion could emotionally throw at me with the support of those who cared for me as deeply as they professed, I simply stated, "I guess it's a good thing that you are *not* the suspicious type then, isn't it, My Friend?"

Relieved at my answer, and especially in the way I had delivered it with some of my old verve returning, he replied "Yes, I believe it is."

Early the next morning, we prepared to depart. Bryce would drive the main coach, with The Duke and Duchess plus the boys as passengers. Meanwhile, Nanny Kaye would have to suffer through the trip with only Sir Preston for company in the coach driven by Chef, as I had decided to ride up top with Bryce.

I can honestly say that there is no better place to be than on top of a carriage while traveling upon a dirt road in the middle of summer if you love dust, sweat, and swearing! It was absolutely *miserable* constantly swaying back and forth to the point of having to hold onto the side rails so as not to fall off. That is until we hit some fantastically deep holes in the road, which caused one to be flung up into the air only to land back down on the hard, wooden carriage seat smacking your backside with enough power to give you a headache. As luck would have it, the road from Arlington Green to Brighton passed through the northern marshes for miles; if one were to count the mosquito bites upon Bryce and myself once we left the marshland behind, they could ascertain how the blood-sucking little terrors most certainly will have a population explosion rather soon.

Stopping every hour or so to stretch our legs and readjust our bouncing parts, it was getting near sunset when we passed a large swath of blackened countryside void of any structures or signs of life. I could hear Tre asking his father what had happened here as his head hung out the window to get a better view of the scorched earth. Spying a small marker posted on the side of the road, Tre called out to Bryce to please stop the carriage so he could read what the marker said and maybe get an understanding of this curiosity.

Pulling over to the side of the road, the carriages emptied as once again legs were stretched allowing the occupants to amble up to the marker and read its message. I did not get down from my perch upon the top of carriage number one to read that sign; I already knew the words by heart. Doing my best to keep a calm exterior even as my insides were in a turmoil, I concentrated on anything I could get my mind set to that would not remind me of what I had experienced here; thus, I did not hear Tre call up to me until he had to repeat himself.

"Dylan, this marker states an unknown Teller-of-Tales helped to save some children at this spot. A friend of yours perhaps?" he asked, his curiosity piqued.

"When one travels upon the road, one learns how every Teller-of-Tales they encounter claims to be that man," I answered truthfully. This explanation must have satisfied him as he got back within the carriage with no further questions or incident.

Rejoining me atop the carriage, Bryce asked why I did not get down with the others and read what message the marker displayed. "Were you not curious about what had occurred in this strange place?" he asked as he took the reins in his hands.

"I've seen it before," was my glum response after which I would say no more.

Three hours later, we rolled into the town of Brighton. As The Duke and his family would be guests of The Earl in his home during The Festival, this was our first stop. We left the members of The Duke's family along with Nanny Kaye, all of their luggage, plus the carriage should it prove to be needed, the horses to be tended by The Earl's capable Stable Master. After a few moments conversation with the man, Bryce appeared satisfied that they would be cared for nearly as well as he himself would have back home in the stables of Arlington Green. Piling onto and into carriage number two, the rest of us found the inn where *we* would be staying. After several ales to wash the road dust from our throats, Bryce and I bid each other a good evening as we retired to our rooms. Later that night, the unmistakable sound of a hard rain pounding upon the window lead me to believe that I would be able to sleep late and probably not miss any of the Festival.

The next morning, as I was prepared to finally climb out of bed, a flash of lightning streaked across the sky closely followed by its nearly simultaneous crash of thunder. Hearing the rain continuing to pour down from the heavens, I knew that the chances of The Festival competition commencing this day were slim to none. Having arrived at this inevitable conclusion, I proceeded to roll over, pull my covers up to my chin, and immediately go back to sleep.

Later that afternoon, as I had dinner with the rest of the men of the Arlington Green Staff, I listened in on some of the conversations swirling around us, most of which dealt with the Festival contestants and their chances of taking the prize. It appeared that there were three favorites whose work I was familiar with deemed capable of winning The Festival. It was when a new addition to the contestants was being discussed that my ears perked up. Apparently, a young female soloist was making people sit up and take notice of her remarkable voice; while she may be a dark horse to win, I was determined to hear her perform and judge her level of talent for myself. Besides, if she were as pretty as they were describing her, I would *definitely* want to see her perform. Inquiring of the gentlemen when this person was scheduled to take the stage, I was told that she would be singing on stage four sometime after the noon hour. Making a mental note to be at stage four well before noontime so as to get an excellent spot to catch her performance, I let the sounds of the storm coupled with the effects of the ales we enjoyed into the night to carry me off to sleep.

The next morning, I awoke to Bryce bellowing that it was time to get out of bed or I would miss the entire event. Noticing the sun shining through the window of my room, I judged that now would indeed be a good time to rise, for surely The Festival must be in full swing. Foregoing the breakfast offered by the inn, I wanted a stomach fully prepared to sample as much and as many different foods as I could before it was time to head toward stage number four. Passing a notice board which was updating when and where the scheduled acts were to perform, we read that because of yesterday's rain, all of today's schedule was set back by several hours in order to fit in those artists cancelled by the storm. Bryce decided that this would be an opportune time to meander down to the barns and see to his horses, so we separated and agreed to meet in three hours' time back at the stage.

There is a scientific something or other which states that if you take dirt—a lot of dirt—and mix it with water—lots and lots of water—you get mud. A *sea* of mud in fact. The fields around the town of Brighton were living proof of this theorem as you could not find a dry patch anywhere.

One of the things in life which I enjoy doing most is sitting back and just watching people; due to the nature of the condition of the fields, I was enjoying myself immensely. Finding a well-placed tree stump on which to position myself, I sat and observed the Brighton version of the Theatre of the Absurd.

Everywhere you looked you could see the tops of boots sticking out of the mud either singly or in pairs—often with the individual attempting to return that footwear onto their feet ending up face up or face down in the mud, right next to their shoe or boot which had refused to budge!

Several young men had gallantly attempted to carry their ladies to keep them from becoming soiled. Naturally, this experiment ended with *both* tumbling into the brown goo. I observed one intrepid soul looking back and forth from the blanket in his arms, which he had brought to lay upon the ground for an intimate picnic lunch with his lady. He looked to the mud, then back to the blanket, then back to the mud no less than ten times, until frustration got the better of him and he threw the blanket down and stormed off with his lady in tow.

I especially felt bad for the women with the nice pretty dresses bought for just this occasion; before long the original colors of their outfits below the knees could not be determined.

Doing my best to keep my merriment from bursting forth, I must not have been doing a very good job of hiding every giggle or guffaw as from behind me I heard, "One could almost assume that the difficulties these poor people are enduring are strictly for your entertainment," a voice heavy with reproach reprimanded me—a very *female* voice. Not knowing if she was alone or in the company of two hulking brutes about to heap a world of destruction upon my person, I slowly turned about upon my stump. Out of sight, I was forming a thick ball of mud with my right hand should the need arise for me to attempt a hasty retreat from two hulking brutes by covering their eyes full of mud!

Luck was shining upon me that day, for when I had turned about to face my antagonist, I saw but one pair of legs encased in trousers that were themselves encased in multiple layers of deep rich brown mud. As I was sitting barely off the ground, naturally my eye level was far from hers, yet I could tell that I was in no danger. Her hands were busy holding up the hem of the dress that she was wearing over those trousers in an attempt to keep it clean. Quickly raising my head so as not to appear rude considering where my eyes were positioned, I found myself looking up into one of the most beautiful faces I had ever seen. Now, if she had not been looking down at me in disgust, I probably could have designated it *the* most beautiful.

Easily!

It is hard to picture fire as well as ice emitting from a pair of the bluest eyes I had ever seen, yet somehow she was proving quite capable of just such a feat. They were accompanied by a set of what would be perfect lips if they weren't presently in the form of a frown. Long blond hair flowed over her shoulders to tumble down halfway to her waist. As I was seemingly in sufficient trouble, I purposely did not allow my eyes to linger viewing her other attributes but made every effort to keep her eyes in view.

The smart retort which had been forming in my mind died upon my lips. I discovered that, somehow, the vision standing before me had caused me to lose my voice entirely! Sensing that if I should remain gazing upon her features it probably would be winter before I was able to find the words to answer her, I forced my eyes down to the ground. After what seemed like an eternity, I could finally mumble something about not meaning any harm, as in reality I was not finding humor in anyone's difficulties.

"Doubtlessly the clouds in the sky are formed in extraordinary funny shapes then," she observed in just the perfect combination of sarcasm and disbelief.

Noticing a heavy up-swell in the number of people walking by where the two of us were currently greatly enjoying each other's company (I am pretty good at that sarcasm thing as well), I rose to my feet and offered her the stump to stand upon so that she would not get splatters upon her dress from the boots of the crowd coming our way.

Her features softened when she realized what I had just offered and why. The smallest of smiles built upon those lips of hers until she remembered that she was supposed to find me reprehensible, at which point it disappeared like a puff of smoke. Offering her my hand to allow her to climb up, the smile returned wider than before making her appear even more beautiful—if that was possible. Thanking me for the kindness, when both of her feet upon the stump, our eyes were at perfect levels with the other's, allowing for a most enjoyable moment when time itself seemed to stand still. All noise and motion emanating from around our one little stump ceased to exist as our eyes remained locked, until we both forced our gazes elsewhere with cheeks red from embarrassment.

There was something so maddeningly familiar about this girl—as if I had known her all my life. Yet, as I was certain that I had never laid eyes upon her before this day, how could this be possible?

Feeling the need to speak, I commented that it was very clever of her to wear the trousers under the dress so as to keep it as free of mud as was possible.

Answering that it was the only thing she could think of in order to get from where she was staying to the stages, I took what was for me an extraordinary risk. I inquired if she would care to accompany me to go listen to some of the music, I would offer to carry her upon my back.

I could actually detect reluctance on her part when she told me it would not be possible.

Shocked how my mouth had formed actual words while my brain was in its usual panic mode when in the presence of a woman, especially one as stunning as the one standing before me, I beat a hasty retreat and acknowledged that it was a very lucky fellow indeed who she was meeting. Bidding her a good day, I took a step to leave when I realized that my hand still encompassed hers—apparently neither one of us had been in a hurry to let go.

There has been a very disturbing tendency in my life (among many I assure you) which seems to require that when something marvelous or wonderful occurs, that something equally terrible is lurking right around the corner waiting to pounce. This once again proved to be true as the continued clasping of our hands initiated the slipping of feet resulting in me landing flat on my back in the mud with her splashing in face-first right next to me!

Shock was registering upon both of our faces—or at least what could be *seen* of our faces, as mud was clinging to my back, her front, and plenty of places in between. Scrambling to our feet proved difficult. No less than three times did one or the other slip back into the goo, until *all* of our sides were now well-covered. Strangely enough, only my hat, which had fallen upon my face, was spared becoming a different shade of brown entirely.

Finally re-gaining our footing, she proceeded to fling off as much mud off of her as she could by flicking her arms down almost as a bird would flap its wing during takeoff. Neither one of us took the other to task because it was impossible to determine just who had caused the emotional commotion with their motion. (Hey, that was pretty good!)

As all of the cloth she was wearing was covered, I did my best to clean the worst of the mud from her face with my hat, but my clumsy attempts at being gentle must not have been going well. Tears began to flow freely from her eyes to mix with the mud that I was smearing more than clearing. Apologizing for doing such a terrible job did nothing to keep her from breaking out into deep mournful sobs. I was utterly frustrated by not knowing if I were better off leaving her alone, or if *she* would be better off if I left her alone, or whether it would be helpful to either of us if I stayed. I determined that until she either told me to leave or actually threw something at me as a sign, I would remain at her side and do anything I could to assist this damsel by attempting to keep her from falling deeper into her doldrums.

My heart was breaking seeing her tiny frame shudder from crying uncontrollably, when I heard the sound of laughter directly behind me. Spotting out of the corner of my eye two young "gentlemen" who had remained clean pointing at us and laughing, I "accidently" stuck out my foot. This resulted in two very surprised young dandies ending up spitting mud from their mouths, which had foolishly remained opened in surprise as their faces became planted in a full six inches of the stuff.

Now if I had been able to do so without losing my *own* footing and ending up in exactly the same spot I had just been able to extricate myself from with great difficulty…

When I regained my feet once again, the young lady continued to shudder, only now it was accompanied by the beginnings of a quiet giggling and smiling tear-free eyes.

"Funny looking clouds?" I asked while doing my best to clear mud from my ears, at which point she burst into full, heartfelt laughter. For several moments we just stood there gazing upon each other and laughing like children. Unfortunately, the mood changed all too quickly as she looked down upon the ruins of her dress; her beautiful smile was once again replaced by despair.

"The offer to carry you so you won't get your dress dirty still stands," I quipped in an attempt to keep her from the despair she was slipping back into. "I will set you back down out of sight of whichever lucky fellow you are meeting," I promised, becoming dejected the moment I said it as a sinking feeling began to gnaw away in my stomach. Why this girl was having the effect upon me to the extent she was I could not discern; all I knew was that she was.

"No, that will not be necessary—although yours was a wonderful offer none-the-less," she said as a brief smile once again came to her. "I am not here to meet someone," she told me much to my relief. "In reality, I am scheduled to sing within several hours...*was* scheduled to sing it appears." On the verge of tears, she looked over her appearance with mounting frustration.

"Well then, allow me to accompany you to where you are staying," I cheerfully suggested. "Get yourself cleaned up, put on a new outfit, and the offer of carrying you still stands. There is, however, one caveat this time: you must tell me your name," I said hoping against hope that she would accept my offer. As of yet unable to understand my infatuation with this girl, I was desperate to make a positive impression on her, while keeping us from parting and the danger of never seeing each other again.

"You know, you really are very sweet...when you aren't laughing at people that is," she admitted while wringing mud from her hair. "My name is Robyn, and while I wish I *could* agree to your offer, I am reluctant to admit how this was the only dress I have decent enough for the stage. It is obviously beyond ruined, which I am certain is how I must appear as well."

Watching as the dejected slow shaking of her head back and forth caused small globs of goo to fly off of her hair to fall back to the earth, I recognized this as one of those "if only" moments. If only that mud had remained on the ground where it should have in the first place, she would have been saved a world of trouble—as well as had the opportunity to possibly make a name for herself.

I heard the words neither of us wanted to hear as she proceeded to tell me that she would have no choice but to withdraw her name from the competition.

Normally by this point, I would have found a reason to bid a hasty retreat from her company and cease the inner turmoil encompassing me while in the close presence of a woman as beautiful as I found her to be. Later on, when I was done berating myself for having acted the coward, I would have justified to myself that someone as beautiful as her would most certainly have no interest in someone such as I. And yet—there was something *so special* about her that I found myself unable to abandon her under the circumstances. Help her I would, and let her reject me later, I decided.

"Robyn, my name is Dylan. While I will gladly profess in depth how glad I am to have met you over dinner this evening if you are so inclined, we have to hurry to get you to an emporium right now. There you can purchase whatever you require to enable you to keep your appointment upon yon stage, and thus save hundreds of people from disappointment!" I said as I took her hand once again and prepared to leave the relative sanctuary of our stump. The only problem was, she was not in any hurry to leave.

"Once again you prove yourself to be a kind fellow," she said, casting her eyes upon the ground as if embarrassed. "I am ashamed to admit such, but I had spent nearly the last money I had in order to buy this one. The life of a poor Singer-of-Songs is not one to be envied."

"Robyn, the poor Teller-of-Tales understands as well as identifies with the poor Singer-of-Songs all too well," I agreed. "Were my pockets full of other than fresh mud, we could rectify this problem right away." I truly was sorry that I was unable to help this young lady. Yet I had just met her, and under less than perfect circumstances. Why would I care so deeply about a perfect stranger?

Because she *was* perfect perhaps?

Or was it because I was so certain that I had seen her before? She found me staring at her in an effort to clear the fog in my head and find an answer.

That...and I liked it, too.

Her cheeks turned the loveliest shade of red in between splotches of dried mud as she blushed when she noted my attention. "Is there still mud on my face?" she inquired while reaching for my hat.

"All over it, I am afraid," I replied honestly. "I am sorry if I have embarrassed you by my staring. It is just that I could swear I have seen you before and am trying to sift through my memories in order to discover the answer to my quandary. Besides," I told her as I took what for me was a bold step indeed, "I find the experience most enjoyable."

Averting her eyes from mine, her blush deepened to encompass most of her face. "I do not see how either of us could have encountered the other, for the road is a large place, indeed," she said while shaking her head as her eyes remained focused upon the ground at our feet. "I am positive that this encounter today is a first, for I most certainly would have recognized you," she offered while raising her head.

Our eyes met, and once again, it was as if everything else in the world disappeared. I cared for nothing else at this moment...all the riches in the world could not tempt me to look away. All that I saw was beauty; all that I saw was her.

A large boisterous group of revelers passing close by broke the spell. Returning to the real world once again, her thinking re-focused upon the cruel reality of her situation.

"This is probably all for the best," she said with a sigh. "I have been naught but *dreadfully* nervous at the thought of being up on that stage. I have performed to smaller audiences a number of times and even this had virtually terrified me," she admitted. Obviously embarrassed, her cheeks returned to a now-familiar rosy red. "To have *hundreds* of eyes and ears wanting to be entertained, only to be disappointed by my nervousness, is something which I have dwelled upon nearly every waking moment of the past few weeks. I never would have won—I'm really not very good, you know."

Hearing words she must have rehearsed in her head until she had begun to believe them to be true, I felt as though I was experiencing the reasoning of a kindred spirit. Here was someone who lacked the personal confidence to see herself apart from the reality she had created.

Recalling all of the arguments given to me by others when I professed the very same lack of confidence which appeared to be overcoming her, I gave her those retorts which I had heard and considered to have moved me the most. Realizing how, more often than naught, this encouragement had been offered since my arrival at Arlington Green, the answer to her predicament came to me in a flash!

"Robyn, you are going to keep your date with destiny after all," I announced with an unmistakable air of certainty. Placing my finger to her lips in order to quash any attempt at argument, I told her that I had a solution to the problem, but that she would have to hurry and follow me right away. Searching my eyes in order to give her the answers she desperately sought within my spirit, she must have found something that brought her peace of mind as she carefully stepped down from her perch upon the stump and offered me her hand once again.

Through that sea of slime, we hustled hand in hand—walking at first, then finally running as quickly as we could while doing our best to keep from falling back into the quagmire.

I freely admit that I would have refused admittance into the castle of The Earl of Brighton to two people looking like Robyn and I if I were the Gatekeeper. Fortunately, he dispatched a guard carrying a message once I was able to convince him that I was in the employ of a guest of The Earl's attending The Festival, and that I required an immediate audience with—of all people—The Duchess of Arlington Green.

About fifteen minutes of my nervous pacing, while Robyn sat in the shadows doing her best to ready her voice for her scheduled vocals, finally produced results when The Duchess arrived at the gate accompanied by Nanny Kaye. Seeing my appearance, The Duchess instantly broke out in hysterical laughing.

Prefacing my story with, "See some funny clouds, My Lady?" which she could not possibly have understood brought about a tiny laugh from Robyn's place among the shadows. I rapidly explained the events of the morning and asked if she would consider alleviating Robyn's predicament by lending me an advance on my salary so I could purchase a new dress (an unbelievable irony as I look back upon the memory of this day, but that is another story for a later time). Motioning for Robyn to step out and join us, she sheepishly appeared in spite of obviously being neither comfortable around nor familiar with members of The Nobility and not know how she was going to be received, especially in the condition she was presently in.

One glance at the pitiful creature standing before her, bowing with her hand in mine for support, The Duchess (to my greatest surprise) announced that no, she would *not* be advancing me any salary!

To *Robyn's* greatest surprise, The Duchess said it would not be necessary as she was certain a proper dress which would fit nicely was surely to be found in the castle. Motioning for the Gatekeeper to open the portcullis, The Duchess took a highly surprised Robyn's hand from mine and asked Kaye to hurry back inside to have a bath drawn.

I could not place the meaning of the look I was receiving from The Duchess as she began to lead Robyn away to get ready for her performance. Could it have been respect or even pride, perhaps?

Yet I could certainly read the expression of appreciation upon the Face of Robyn—at least the part not still covered in mud.

Remaining in place to watch the two women walking across the courtyard, I could not stop grinning from ear to ear, for I was enjoying a heaping helping of feeling immensely happy—that is until I heard Robyn answering The Duchess's question of how she knew me by saying that we had just met several hours prior. To an accompanying laugh, a very amused Duchess replied, "This would explain why you are still willing to hold his hand!" after which they disappeared into the castle doorway.

Beautiful Voices...
Beautiful Singers

Standing in a quagmire halfway up to my knees, I was not willing to (nor able to frankly) move from my place directly in front of stage number four. I waited outside the Earl's front gate until I received a message from The Duchess that Robyn would be performing on stage four at a certain time, and to please go away as I was making the Gatekeeper nervous! I wandered about The Festival for several hours and filled my belly with all kinds of tasty treats. Figuring that I could not only catch Robyn's performance but also get the chance to hear the new act which I had heard such excitement for at the inn last night, I was content to keep my place while suffering through several groups or soloists who thought themselves capable of carrying a tune and failing miserably in the attempt.

Thinking that perhaps they should screen the acts wishing to perform to determine quality, I immediately threw that thought from my mind. Did not Robyn say she was not very good? If this was indeed the case, then she possibly would not have been here at all and I never would have met her. Not that there would be much, if any, time to spend together in the several days before I was to be leaving for Arlington Green. The best I was hoping for was to get up enough daring and ask her if she would consider visiting me during her travels. I had actually considered going back on the road as a way of meeting up with her but had dismissed that notion as impractical for my nice comfy bed is too heavy to carry upon my shoulders. Besides, who knows if she would even welcome my company?

I have never had very much luck with relationships. Okay, I have had *none* and quite frankly have virtually given up on that aspect of my life. I am a good fellow at heart and not out to hurt or take advantage of anyone, *especially* a young lady to whom I am attracted. My problem—if this is not too far beyond the realm of possibility and belief—is my mouth! I have a way about myself which is very noticeable to anyone having spent enough time in my presence. I have a certain need to hide most of myself behind trying to be clever and funny until I become familiar with an individual and build up a trust in them. It is then that I can begin to open up and let my real self be known.

The trouble with this aspect of my personality is that women whom I have known—and there have not been very many of those, are generally not willing to invest the time or effort getting through the exterior nonsense until they can discover the inner me and determine if the effort was worth the cost.

I had vacillated for the past two hours between the notion that Robyn might actually be interested in me and wondering how such a miracle would be even possible. I'm certain she was appreciative to me for the assistance I gave her, but there is a great chasm between appreciation and romantic interest. When I picture her outward beauty in my mind, I realized I had no chance for it would take some mighty powerful inner beauty to be willing to settle for someone like me. Finally, assured that she undoubtedly had a line of suitors a mile long, there had to be many young fellows she could choose much better than I.

Yeah, but maybe…

Fortunately, the arrival of Bryce kept me from driving myself permanently insane!

Bryce suggested that remaining in this damnable sea of mud was not in our best interests and there were some ales back at the inn calling for us, but I told him I had to stay and could catch up with him later. When he asked what could possibly be so important that I was willing to risk permanently wrinkled feet and toes, I explained the events of the day since we had separated. Telling him how I *had* to stay and hear Robyn sing (as well as see how beautiful she actually was free of dirt and mud), he admitted that he had always been a great fan of wrinkly feet and took up a place to wait next to me.

He did make a big mistake however; he asked me to tell him about this girl I was so anxious to see once again and hear perform.

Big mistake!

For the next half-hour I carried on using every superlative I could find in my vocabulary to describe her beauty. I recalled every word of our conversation—twice, then asked if he thought that a girl like her could possibly be interested in someone like me. All the while, I was straining my neck so as to spot her when she made her way through the crowd towards the stage.

Not waiting for his answer, I once again began to describe her as I had discovered some superlatives which I had failed to use earlier when I noticed him reaching down into the mud and bring up a ball of such in his hand. When I asked him what that ball was for, he replied how it was meant for me and would be shoved down my back if I did not be quiet for at least a minute's time!

I did my best to comply. I really did! Fifteen seconds was as long as I could hold out; besides I figured that he was bluffing.

He wasn't.

It was when I never even tried to remove the goo that he became impressed. "She must be very special indeed," he observed. "I have never seen you act this way. Perhaps she prefers taller and more muscular men?"

"Only in order for her to step over their lifeless bodies in hopes of keeping her dress clean," I answered flatly.

"Okay Brother," he laughed while slapping me on the back. "I will be good and see if your taste in women exceeds my expectations." Now if only he could have done so *without* smashing the ball of mud he had put there earlier.

His light-hearted demeanor changed instantly as he must have spotted something that caused him great concern. "He'd better be taking good care of them!" he muttered under his breath as he gazed at a spot behind the stage itself. "If he even so much as laid a whip upon their backs, I swear he will wish this day had never been."

The object of his concern were his own horses which were pulling the coach belonging to The Duke and Duchess up to the rear of the stage. Fortunately, the groom handling the reins had skill and brought the coach to a gradual and easy stop indicating his ability and love for horses to a degree acceptable to Bryce. From the side of the carriage facing us, The Duke and Duchess appeared, while Nanny Kaye exited the other side with someone covered by several cloaks. Assuming this person to be the Earl's wife, I went back to searching for Robyn's arrival as I wanted to give her some last-minute encouragement.

The setting of the stage was such that while us unimportant people got to stand in the mud, extended covered bench seating reserved for the people of means built up off the ground assured them that they would remain comfortable and debris-free, while showing off their finery for all to see. Watching as they took their places amongst the other Nobles or people of wealth, I saw The Duchess peering out over the hundreds of music enthusiasts awaiting the next act when she spotted Bryce and myself. Satisfied that we had indeed made it into the audience, she settled back into her seat soon to be joined by Nanny Kaye.

Of the Lady of Brighton, there was no sign.

I was tempted to have Bryce save my spot so I could make my way through the crowd and inquire of The Duchess when Robyn would be arriving, but at that moment the Master of Ceremonies came out from behind the curtains to announce the next act to perform. As it was the name I recognized as the girl who was spoken of so highly by the group in the inn last night, I remained where I was, figuring I could go inquire of The Duchess after the performance was finished.

The curtains slowly parted to reveal a single chair placed in the center of the stage. Turning to face Bryce, I reminded him that this was the act supposed to be so good, when I heard applause break out from among the crowd indicating someone had stepped out onto the stage. Turning back in order to see the object of their applause, I could not believe my eyes—for seated upon the chair, with lyre in hand, was none other than Robyn!

There had to be some mistake. This was not who had been announced; this was a girl named Robyn about to perform. A most beautiful girl named Robyn, I might add! Not only had she been able to clean off the mud and dirt, she was dressed in a very stylish dress the likes of which she would never have been able to afford. A string of pearls adorned her neck, with what I assumed to be matching earrings dangled from her ears. Her head swept back and forth as if searching through the audience, until she spotted where I stood. Breaking out into the happiest of smiles, she actually started giggling while holding her hands up to her dress as if to say, "*Can you believe this!*"

Sharing in her happiness, I offered her the magnanimous gesture of removing my hat while bowing low. Standing back up, my elbow was introduced to the solar plexus of one Bryce Willis as he made what I considered a comment most unworthy regarding the vision of beauty seated upon that stage. Doubled over as he was, he gave me a look of confusion (coupled with pain, I am happy to add) to which I whispered, "It is her!"

"I know," he grunted as he stood back up. "This is the girl whom you wanted so badly to hear. How does that rate me a poke in the belly?"

"No, you don't understand," I exclaimed as my excitement at hearing her sing could not be kept within. "*This* is Robyn!"

"Brother," he said while looking back upon the stage, "your descriptions did not do her justice."

Gesturing to her that she should just look into my eyes as a method for not seeing the audience and thus becoming nervous at their size, she gestured back that I should look at the smile she was beaming my way.

By now the applause had stopped. Setting the lyre upon her lap she said, "Thank you for your warm greeting," in a shaky voice indicating the degree of nervousness she must be experiencing. I found myself praying that she would provide a capable performance, for crowds can be most cruel to those who perform with their hearts but cannot support the effort with talent. Thankful that Bryce was here to protect my back in case I attacked the first person to boo or howl, it soon become obvious such bold actions would not be required, as with a strumming of her lyre and with voice still shaky yet growing in power by the note, she proceeded to destroy any misgivings I may have had regarding her talents.

She was magnificent! Her notes were always in tune, while the range of her voice exceeded any which I had heard previously. The playing of her lyre, blended with her singing, made one question whether an angel had escaped from the heavens to entertain us mere mortals with such beauty the likes of which was destined never to be seen nor heard again upon this earth.

Not very good my ass.

As if time itself stopped, the crowd was mesmerized—literally frozen motionless as the last notes of her song were carried away by the wind. All too soon it was over. Absolute silence greeted her once her last note was performed. She stood slowly, as if expecting to hear the sounds of dissatisfaction blasting her ears from a mostly unhappy audience.

Appearing to wake from a lovely dream, the audience's applause grew slowly until it was thunderous in volume. A beaming Robyn took her bow, and another, and yet *another* while the intensity of the clapping of hands would not diminish. I watched as she wiped a tear from her eye, she was so moved by the reaction to her efforts. I could feel her eyes meet mine, almost as if a connection had just been made the likes of which could stand the test of time.

Or so I hoped.

Due to the rain delaying the progression of the acts scheduled to perform, only one song was allowed per artist to assure that all the acts scheduled would be capable of performing. This did not sit well with the audience what-so-ever. Howls of displeasure greeted the Master of Ceremonies as he re-appeared to lead Robyn off stage. Anxious to see her and tell her how proud of her I was and what a fantastic performance she gave, I turned to Bryce to make a comment when my words died in my throat.

Surprise turned to disbelief and then to shock, for off in the crowd, I recognized a face which I had never expected to see ever again. The last time I had laid eyes upon that countenance, he had been walking off into the face of a blizzard after having saved my life on the night of Holiday Eve. A most pleasant smile met my eyes as he noticed me looking his way—and then he was gone.

With the intensity of a madman I plunged into the crowd in an effort to catch up with him, leaving a very stunned Bryce behind. Pushing and shoving, I grabbed person after person in an attempt to reach him before he could disappear on me once again. Spying him every minute or so, I forced my way onward yet could never seem to make any headway in closing the distance between us. Soon I had left stage four completely behind as I blindly followed his trail. So focused upon my determination to speak with him, I completely forgot about a certain young lady who should be receiving accolades unending from me at this moment.

Seeing him momentarily paused by a message board, he once again managed to meet my gaze. A familiar smile was the last of him I saw as he once again disappeared from view, this time for good. I hurried to the spot where I had seen him last, yet any sign of his presence in the crowd further eluded me. A deep sadness overcame me as I had so wanted to see him again and hear his words; perhaps in this way, I would find the inner strength to pass by the grave of Brackensburg without fear and turmoil.

Thank God for Robyn, for her presence had driven away the unrelenting torment I had been experiencing in knowing that we would have to pass that damnable cursed ground upon our return journey. I could only hope I was capable of passing within sight of where the chapel had stood without being in real danger of losing my mind.

Reluctantly I was prepared to make my way back to stage four when my eyes happened to stray onto the message board which he obviously had wanted me to find. Having read the words once, I paused in disbelief as I read them once more. With a sudden intensity similar to that which I had displayed in my recent chase, I plunged into the crowd once again in search of stage three. How I did not slip and fall many times over as I hurried as quickly as I was able I could not say.

Arriving out of breath in front of stage three, I had arrived just in time as a different announcer came through the closed curtain to introduce the next group to take the stage.

"Ladies and gentlemen," he began, his voice loud enough to carry throughout the crowd. "There are many various performers this season at the Festival of Music. Some are better than others, I will warrant. I do believe that you would be hard-pressed to find a group the likes of which I am about to introduce to you now. The obstacles which they have overcome just to be here are nothing short of a miracle. They are without doubt the bravest group of children you could ever hope to meet. Ladies and gentlemen," he intoned as the curtains began to open "it is my pleasure to introduce to you...*The Sixteen Children of the Rope*."

It was them!

They had grown taller of course. Some of the older ones exhibited the distinct outward signs of reaching the early stages of adulthood, but it was them. The sixteen little children who I lead from the hellhole of Brackensburg that night waited a scant few feet away from where I stood transfixed as if in a dream. When they began to sing, I burst out in tears not caring who thought it to be strange.

Once more, I heard their familiar little voices singing the very song I had taught them that had carried their courage all the way to Brighton. Light as a feather, my heart soared as I gazed upon the faces of sixteen young souls who would not have been saved had it not been for the strength and courage of Padre Bartholomew...as well as myself.

As if in the back of my mind, I could once again hear the words of the Mysterious Stranger spoken from around the fire on that most special Holiday Eve. *"Listen to the children sing."*

Peace came to my soul as I knew I would finally be free of any more turmoil from the ghosts of Brackensburg for all time.

I was so tempted to rush upon that stage and join them in their singing. Instead, I quietly sang it with them from my place in the audience. Waiting until they had concluded their song and the last one had walked off the stage, I slowly made my way back as if in a daze to where I thought Bryce would be waiting for me at stage four.

When I had gotten back, he was not to be seen until I looked over in the direction of where The Duke and Duchess had been seated. I spied him seated atop their coach. Apparently, he did not fully trust their groom and was going to drive the carriage back to the stables himself. Standing outside of the carriage as if waiting for someone I spotted The Duchess,

Nanny Kaye, and—oh my God! The figure of Robyn stood out from the rest, her head as if on a swivel constantly searching for me.

In the magic of the moment, I had inexplicably forgotten her and her performance. I can only imagine (or at least *hope*) that she had anxiously looked for me in order to share in the happiness she must have been feeling, not only for the reception her performance had received, but especially for her triumph over her fears at being on stage. No matter how many superlatives I could weave now, it would never be the same as sharing a moment which had passed forever. And I could not even explain my bizarre behavior as a means of justifying leaving her as I did.

As I approached closer, if I had any doubts regarding how my return would be viewed, the expressions on the faces of both The Duchess as well as Nanny Kaye made it obvious that I would be lucky to survive.

It is amazing just how quickly you can go from experiencing heaven to catching hell!

Gathering up all of my courage, I continued to approach, my focus only for the beauty which was Robyn when she spied me and our eyes met. While I still received a sweet smile, it was nowhere near the reception I could have experienced had I been there to share in her moment of triumph.

Ignoring the looks of pure disgust that I received from the other two ladies, I walked up to where Robyn stood and took both of her hands in mine. I proceeded to tell her all that I was feeling, from how magnificent her performance was to how proud I was of her for having the courage to overcome her fears. I saved how beautiful she looked as she performed for last, adding how I did not think it possible but that she was even more captivating when I saw her up close. She did not make to remove her hands from mine—this little act was performed very capably by The Duchess. Now that she finally had my attention, she proceeded to inquire which side of the Stupid Tree I had been born under?

It went downhill very quickly from there.

In the next ten minutes of so (it may have been an hour for all I know) I was berated in front of the girl I was worried about being able to properly impress. Did mud seep in through my ears in sufficient quantities to assure that I couldn't think straight, I was asked. What in heaven's name was I thinking (an interesting question under the circumstances), to which Nanny Kaye piped in that I obviously *wasn't* thinking. No less than a dozen times did I hear the expression "this poor girl" immediately followed up by "How could you be so insensitive?" Finally, the ultimate question surfaced when The Duchess demanded, "Pray tell us what was so important you had to rush off at just that moment and where the hell *did* you go?"

"My Lady," I said when I finally received the chance to speak, "I respectfully say that I cannot answer your question." This did no good at all in alleviating her demands.

"Can't answer or won't?" she inquired angrily.

"Regardless of which the case may be, I cannot tell you the answer you seek," I informed her in a way which let her know she would not be receiving the information she wanted.

Getting right up into my face, she whispered quietly so only the two of us could hear. "And you were doing so well. How could you throw it all away?"

Turning towards Robyn, The Duchess suggested that she should accompany them back to the Castle, where the Gatekeeper would be informed that under no circumstances would I be allowed inside and thus be able to bother her any longer.

Robyn tried to read what lay behind my eyes in order to discern which was the real Dylan: the one who went out of his way for her to be able to perform, or the one who was nowhere to be found when it came time to celebrate her success. Apparently Robyn had made up her mind as she turned to face The Duchess and asked if it was acceptable, then she would remain behind for a time all the same.

"I suppose everyone is entitled to a mistake, Dear," The Duchess said as she made to board the carriage. "When you have finished wasting your time with this one, come up to the castle where we can celebrate your efforts properly."

Before the carriage departed, I caught a glance from Bryce up on top which promised that it would be his turn soon enough to inform me what an idiot I am.

Hugging her sides as if to protect herself, Robyn wondered why The Duchess would be inviting her to join them up at the Castle when they had only met her a scant few hours prior.

"Because she is who she is," I said. Just because The Duchess viewed me as being lower than the bottom of a gopher's hole at the moment didn't mean I thought any less of her. After all, consider how she had transformed a Robyn covered in mud and debris into the stunning creature standing before me.

"You conceal your anger for her rather well," she commented, thinking she understood the situation while attempting to discover if she was reading me correctly.

"You could not be more wrong," I explained as we began to slowly walk along the path away from the staging area and its sea of brown goo. "I have no anger towards her for what she had said just now. It turns out that she is right: I *am* a fool for not being there when you got off stage. I can think of few things more enjoyable than seeing you flush with excitement at just that moment, and I cannot apologize enough for not being there to share such with you. That is, if you even wanted me to be," I stammered, the unsure Dylan who was afraid of rejection rearing his ugly head once more in the face of a beautiful girl.

Realizing that I was proceeding solely on my own, I stopped and turned to find Robyn standing in the middle of the path with a look of pure amazement upon her face. A light breeze was beginning to build, causing her hair to blow about her face but not sufficiently to hide her expression from registering upon me. "Are you serious?" was all that she asked.

As I was in unfamiliar territory, I asked her was I serious about which part?

"Are you purposely trying to get rid of me?" she now wondered, her own confusion causing her to misunderstand me while showing the beginnings of anger. "For if that is so, you could have at least had the good graces to tell me before the carriage left!"

"Robyn, please. I know from having just met this day how you do not know me well and cannot discern when I am in earnest, but you must trust me when I say that nothing could be further from my desire. If you must know the truth, it is not often that I find myself in the company of so beautiful a woman as I see standing before me," I attempted to explain. "Actually, were I to be *completely* honest, it is not often I find myself in the company of *any* woman who has shown an interest in me, and as such I am experiencing difficulties with trying to think of *what* to say."

"A Teller-of-Tales without words?" she asked somewhat amazed.

"Such is the effect you have upon me," I admitted as I gave her a shy smile.

I had forgotten just how beautiful she was when she smiled!

"You must forgive me for mistrusting you," she said as she began walking with me once again. "Traveling as much as I do, I have developed a very strong method of protecting myself by searching for justifications for mistrust, even when upon occasion they do not exist. Normally, I am rather good at determining the honor and integrity of an individual. Yet if this ability can be used with you, I cannot fully decide," she admitted as we slowly meandered along. "One moment I see a fellow who has taken what appears to be more than a passing fancy with me. This fellow shares in my poverty yet is willing to forego future payment for his efforts by asking if his resources could be used to assist me in my hour of need when he has no requirement to do so. These are the signs indicating a man who is considerate and compassionate. And yet" (why does there always have to be an 'and yet' following some good words about me?) "at the very moment when I am the happiest I have been in many a day, he disappears as if concerned for neither my feelings nor my success! How do I read you Dylan?"

She asked this cautiously, apparently striving within herself to decide who I really was. "Is the man I see before me the caring man capable of showing love and worthy of receiving the same in return? Or was The Duchess right in her assessment when she stated that you were a selfish clod incapable of caring for anyone but himself? Why do you have to be so difficult to understand?" she lamented, all the while not aware how many others had gone before her wondering just the very same thing.

Frantically searching for what magic words I could use to convince her how she could believe in me when in truth I did not believe in myself, I did my best to rally my thoughts.

"Robyn, this morning you did not know me at all," I began as I hoped against all hope for success as I really did care for this girl—cared for her a lot! "Only you are capable of determining whether you were better off this morning…or have these few hours we have spent together brought you a promise of happiness which can only be measured in the heart? I cannot answer this for you. I certainly wish that I could, for then I would know if what I feel for you was within you also, and if you would be willing to return the same to me," I said, exposing my greatest fear. "For me to be able to pull aside the curtains I have drawn around me these many years and give you the power to tear my heart to pieces, should I even be able to free the restrictions I have placed upon myself, is a question which I cannot answer. But what I *can* tell you with a certainty is this: I am most willing to take this risk should you be of similar mind." I told her this just as I realized that I had already begun to break down my restrictive barriers regardless of her answer.

"I could offer you assurances and promises that I am indeed worthy of your trust, but what would they be but words hollow and empty of content unless you could read my mind and know for a certainty my heart," I explained, wondering if I was convincing her of my honest intentions or giving her reasons to run from me as fast as she could. "Perhaps you would consider this: did I do my best to procure an outfit for you to wear for the competition for my own personal gain? Or was the opportunity for you to perform guaranteed you by a man eager to see that you lived your dream for a moment capable of lasting a lifetime? You claimed to not be very good and I assumed you would never have this same opportunity again. Which brings up a very interesting point—why *did* you lie to me about the level of your talent?" I asked in a way which indicated a sense of mistrust caused solely by her actions. "And why did you never tell me how you had created a stage name for yourself? You must have known that I would discover your fabrication. Or perhaps you were willing to appear under false pretenses and not care how I would react when I discovered that I had been lied to?"

I could not believe that I had just spoken those words to her! Perhaps my defenses had taken over when they sensed I was exceeding their protective screen? Unfortunately, wishing that one could go back and re-do this day, thus eliminating the many mistakes shared by the both of us, accomplished nothing.

Hanging her head so as not to look at me, she confided how her estimation of her ability had *been* no lie, for that is how she truly saw herself. "As to the ruse with the name, I did not think it important, for many girls whose lives center upon incessant travel from town to town do so under names other than their own. I believed this to be common knowledge—especially by one whose *extensive* travels on the road *must* have left him far more intelligent than the common man!" she declared as the anger in *her* voice rose with every word spoken. "You want to talk about truth versus fabrications? Then tell me Dylan, why you were not there to share in my moment—and where *did* you go?"

On the chess board of love, I had just been checkmated. I could not share what I had experienced, for who would believe such a tale? As for the children, I had taken a vow not to speak about my experiences or brag about what I had done that night, so how could I possibly explain my actions? I knew what I had hoped for would be dashed into tiny irretrievable pieces the moment I said what I was about to. The level of pain I was experiencing due to this knowledge was excruciating, yet I could not say other than what I did.

"I'm sorry, but I cannot share it with you," I told her flatly, the sad realization that I had been right evident in her eyes.

"Then I guess that as neither of us truly trusts the other, I will bid you goodbye, and thank you so very much for helping me realize my dream—even if it *has* turned into a nightmare!" she said as with tears in her eyes, she turned in the other direction and began walking out of my life.

Never have I been so miserable in my entire lifetime! Taking one look at me as I sat in the inn downing ale upon ale, Bryce decided how the tongue-lashing which he had refined all afternoon had best not be shared. Instead, this man who was probably my first and only true friend quietly sat down next to me with an ale in each hand. "If you wish to talk, I am available to listen without judgement," he said while working up a small smile.

Honestly touched by his consideration, I was able to manufacture a rough smile of my own. "Thank you, My Friend," I replied, very happy that he was there. "I say let's find that magical place where thoughts cannot tread and memories fade from all knowledge."

The next day, I did not bother to go hear any more singers performing at The Festival as the roaring in my head would not cease. In fact, I neither left my room all day nor wanted to if the truth be known. In spite of a lifetime of attempts, I still had yet to learn how I could not hide from myself.

Day two found me to be of the same motivation, as I was willing to simply wait around until the next morning's sunrise when we would be departing for home. After tomorrow, I would have the opportunity of pondering what *could* have been for the rest of my life.

It was just about midday when a knock on the door broke the spell I had put myself into. Not wishing to see *anyone* much less talk about "that woman", I rolled over in my bed to face the wall and wait for them to go away.

Whoever was on the other side of that door was persistent indeed, as they refused to go away and kept up that unending knocking until finally I had enough. Grumbling about "Why can't you leave me the hell alone whoever you are," with heart full of anger, I slid out of bed and threw open the door.

The cursing I had readied for the inspired knocker died upon my lips as I found myself face to face with of all people—The Duke.

"Would you care to come downstairs and share a cup with me, or should I come in?" he asked in a way that I knew I was not about to be left alone. Mumbling something about having drunk enough ale to last two lifetimes, I motioned for him to come in.

Entering my room, he looked about. I could sense he was not impressed, but then *I* wasn't staying in a castle, was I? Taking the only chair there, he brought it over to the bed and sat down.

"We've missed you the past two days," he said. "I'd ask you how you were, but as I've already spoken to Bryce, I don't believe those words will be necessary." He searched my face in order to get a read on how deep I was inside myself.

Waiting to see if I offered any response, the silence built until he knew it would be him who would speak.

"For what it's worth, I can certainly understand you acting this way," he told me to my surprise. "I've met the girl—my apologies—I've met

Robyn and she really is very special. Such a sweet spirit and quite attractive, I might add," he told me with a smile on his face and head cocked to one side as he nodded as if in agreement with his statement.

"How have you made such observations?" I wondered after finally deciding to join the conversation. "Have you seen her walking about the grounds with weapons in hand searching for me?"

"Oh no," he replied as he shook his head back and forth for emphasis. "She has been staying at the Castle as a guest of the Earl. What a charming creature she is. The Duchess just loves her." Visions of Robyn entered my mind anew as he spoke of her.

It was an indication of how far I had sunk when I declared, "Well, thank you very much for the opportunity of making me think once again of that which I have lost, Sir. I certainly am glad she is having the time of her life up there with all of you important folks."

I was goading him due to my disparaging state of mind. He knew this to be true as he would not take the bait I had tossed in front of him. "Oh, she is far from having a wonderful time," he confided. "In fact, she is spending most of her days in tears. The Duchess is running out of dresses for her to wear in an effort to get her out of her doldrums."

"You really should go see her," he said in a fatherly tone as if I were Tre or Brandon. "It would do you *both* some good I do believe," he suggested, hopeful I would agree for both of our sakes. When I did not respond he quietly asked, "Couldn't you at least go and tell her goodbye?"

For one brief moment, I heard the voice of The Duke of Arlington Green speaking, yet it was the visage of The Artist I did see sitting across from me. While in many ways both men were as different as night and day, both of them shared a caring and concern for me which I had not experienced since the day my parents failed to return. While I may not have sufficiently expressed my gratitude to The Artist before I left, at this moment

I was determined to never make the same mistake with The Duke. He would readily know my opinions of how much I appreciated him.

Just not at this moment.

He waited me out this time, until I was forced to respond. "Sir, I do appreciate your coming here with your concerns—I truly do. In fact, I find it heart-warming. But I cannot agree with you in how I should go see her, as I can't imagine such a visit would fail to end in confrontation."

Telling me how he had heard about the incident from The Duchess—*over and over* he admitted with the semblance of a grin—he did not claim to understand all of the details. Left to his own speculation, as I would offer nothing from my side to help him gain any insight, he had to eventually agree how I was right. Perhaps it *would* be best for me not to go.

Silence filled the room as neither of us knew what to say. It was him who finally chose to take this conversation where he felt it had to go for my benefit.

"Not to change the subject, but I have to tell you how one of the advantages we have in staying with The Earl is that every night he has some of the acts from The Festival perform for all of his guests. It really is quite entertaining," he offered seemingly at random.

"If you are using that as a ploy to get me there, it really was a very poor try," I informed him, certain of my impression of his attempt.

"Oh no, you misunderstand me, My Boy. I was simply making conversation and had no ulterior motives, I assure you," he said, which I did not fall for. "No, I just wanted to mention the fact how various singers have graced his halls," he claimed, the epitome of virtue and honesty. "In fact, one group performed last night which was very special indeed! It appears that a group of sixteen small children survived the debacle created by their parents in the old Brackensburg. They are called "The Children of the Rope" for some obscure reason."

At the mention of the children, I immediately perked up. He had caught me by surprise and snuck that fact in there. I did not tell him how he was sneaky; his broad smile betrayed this fact.

"They certainly were adorable," he continued on as if he had failed to notice my reaction. "Very good, too. I got a chance to talk to them after their performance as I just *had* to discover the significance of the rope in their story. I'm sure you would have done the same, what with your over-active sense of curiosity and all," he said after which he went into another of his waiting me out until I had to speak deals.

"I would not have been so curious as to pester them after singing," I openly lied.

"No, no...I suppose you would not." His words spoke of agreement, but he knew me too well to fall for that one. "Amazing story about that rope," he continued on with his tale. "It seems how after the local Padre had brought them into their chapel for temporary safekeeping, a traveling Teller-of-Tales brought them out to safety by having them hold onto a piece of rope! It must be true, as the marker we passed on our way to arrive here indicated the same."

"Having read the marker outside of where the town had once stood, I was struck by the fact how the name of a very brave man important to the story was not mentioned," he said as if truly amazed. "I asked the children if they would possibly divulge his name to me—and to a child they refused. They did say how this man had asked only one thing of them after he had personally gotten them safely within the castle walls. His wish was that they never divulge his name to anyone. Now why do you suppose this would be?"

Receiving no reply, he stubbornly continued on. "Yes, that was just the reaction I had received from the children—silence. Believing how I had surmised the answer, it was at this point when I took a chance and stated, 'Now wasn't that just like Dylan, not wanting anyone to know how it was him that night?' I suppose such a tactic was not fair—especially as I was dealing with children," he admitted freely. "Imagine my surprise when several of the younger children answered that yes, it was, before becoming hushed by the older ones!"

He knew! Piece by piece he was bringing the story to me as if playing a game of chess and contemplating his every move.

What an amazing man.

It's just that I wished he was not so amazing and that my secret would remain just that...a secret.

"That's quite a tale you just told," I said as if to change the course of the conversation. "Good tone—excellent use of vocabulary. Perhaps it should be you telling tales within The Manor when we return?" I suggested somewhat sarcastically.

How is it that no matter what I say to him, he never gets angry? Okay, there have been *some* exceptions to such a statement, but as those experiences are not part of this moment, we shall just move on, shall we?

"Oh no, I could never copy *your* talents," he said in response. Once again he had failed to be goaded into something other than his purpose in being there. Becoming very serious, he asked me the question I had been dreading. "Why did you wish to remain anonymous?" he wondered, his confusion and curiosity obvious. "Such a feat as you performed that night was nothing short of miraculous! Why 'The Unknown' moniker?" he wanted to know.

"Because it is my contention that night belonged to Padre Bartholomew and those brave little children," I informed him when I realized how indeed I had no choice. In a way, it felt good to finally get my secret told. Yet I feared that the truth would spread; this I did not want at all.

Promising to keep this knowledge between us, he actually rose and shook my hand. "You have done some good things since you have joined us at Arlington Green," he said in admiration, "but the bravery and skill you demonstrated that night is beyond description! I am so proud of you, My Boy. So *very* proud! And now I know why you were reluctant to come to The Festival."

For the longest time he just stood looking at me, his smile stretching from ear to ear. "It appears that I am a rather good judge of character after all," he beamed in reference to his hiring me.

"Either that or it was those ales talking," I joked, an indication how I might be coming back to what I would consider normal while others might disagree with so lofty an opinion.

"Worry not, your secret is safe with me," I was assured much to my relief. "And the incident with Robyn makes sense now that I understand why you were not present. It was because the children were singing elsewhere at the time. It was a hard choice you were forced to make, My Boy. I'm just so sorry that it may have cost you something special."

"Sir…those *children* are something special," was all I could find to say.

Nodding his head in agreement, he once more took my hand and told me how proud he was of me, after which he reminded me how we were to leave at dawn.

"Bryce will attend to the carriages and the packing. Sleep well, and we shall see you in the morning," he said as he left.

By the next morning, I had finally come to grips with the fact that I probably would never see Robyn again. Anything which *could* have been just was not meant to be. It would take some time to get over her—I knew that to be true, but at least I was able to function once again.

For once I wished how I believed in fate, and that somehow it could have taken over for me when I needed it the most.

Punctual as always, The Duke's carriage came rolling up to the inn just as dawn was breaking. Slinging my bag over my shoulder, I was just about to pull myself up onto the top of the coach when the thought of watching every league of Brighton pass by and taking me away from a certain blond-haired beauty, was more than I could handle. Instead, I slunk into the carriage and closed the flap over the window where I sat in hopes that recollections of this place and especially one person in particular would begin to fade from memory.

Sometime during the journey amidst the incessant bumping and jostling, I fell into an uneasy sleep. Once again, the recurring dreams returned just as vividly as ever. This time, however, there was one major difference to the event.

Startled into sudden waking, I could understand one of the dreams as I never had before. The first remained as confusing as ever, its meaning elusive to me still. It was the second one where I finally gained clarity.

The beautiful woman I have always pictured encountering—the one somehow needing my help? The one I could never get out of my mind as I felt I was meant to meet this woman? For the very first time, I could finally recall her features upon waking.

To my greatest regret, I wish that I could not.

For the lady in my dream...was Robyn!

~ The End ~

The following is an excerpt from book two of the initial trilogy
Tales from the Lands of Arlington Green
"Dylan's Dilemmas"

The aroma wafting from the soiled straw perched upon my shovel was a perfect match for the opinion of what I thought of this latest punishment dealt to me. It mattered not how I had justifiably earned the revolting task of helping clean out the stables several times over for my most recent indiscretions. For a talent such as mine, a hot summer afternoon should be spent down at my favorite fishing spot thinking up new tales and not in the reek which I found myself in up to the tops of my boots.

"Brother, from what I heard, you are lucky to be getting off easy with only *this* punishment to serve," offered my best friend Bryce between his loads of clean straw being strewn over the areas which I had reluctantly just cleared. Being the Master of the Stables, Bryce had the luxury of choosing which of the duties he wished—whether to shovel seemingly endless reeking used straw or clean fresh straw for the horse's bedding. Being a wise young man, he naturally chose the latter.

That and there were more than a few paybacks being delivered this day.

"That's easy for you to say," I countered, ceasing my cleaning efforts to lean on the handle of the shovel. The sting of sweat in my eyes made me wipe the sleeve of my tunic across my brow. Unfortunately, this brought my nose within close proximity of my highly soiled gloves and doing nothing to improve my mood in the least.

It was not that I minded helping out a friend, for such was not my way. What irked me so, and had really gotten under my skin, was the fact that I had gotten caught in the first place. Taking up the handle of the shovel once again, I was about to take my frustrations out on the pile of offal in stall number two when a large rat broke from underneath the pile and ran up my leg! Without thinking, I went to swat the animal off of my trousers with the soiled gloves still on my hands. Before the blow could fall, the rodent jumped off and out into the safety of the barnyard, leaving this Teller-of-Tales cursing a blue streak as I noticed the brown-colored one left behind on my leg for my efforts.

Being the friend that he was, as well as a good man by his nature, Bryce refrained from adding to my exasperation by keeping to himself the laughter which he felt about to explode from within. This was not an easy task to accomplish by any means with the events playing out in front of him.

"And just how is that easy for me to say?" Bryce inquired as a means to get my mind back on task and out of the doldrums I was rapidly sinking into.

"Because you are used to this...this *job*," I explained as I motioned to the stables and its tethered horses about me. "You *chose* this life—whereas I should be outside enjoying the glories of nature, or at the very least the inside of my closed eyelids as I wrestle with a well-deserved nap somewhere in the cool shade," I continued.

"Which is probably where you *would* be," Bryce conceded while trying to be heard over the incessant buzzing of the hundreds of flies that called the stable home, "if you hadn't gone and done something stupid to raise The Duchess's ire yet again."

A far-off look came to my face only to be replaced by an impish grin as I recalled just what had been done to earn me this trip to the stables.

Knowing how he would never be able to break my spirit or at the very least convince me why I should at least *consider* growing up, Bryce warned

"You had better be careful, Brother. One of these days you're going to push them too far—and then where will you be?" he asked as if to make me see reason.

Remembering my experiences as a wandering Teller-of-Tales before coming under the employment of The Duke and Duchess made me stop and honestly contemplate Bryce's advice. Deep down I knew Bryce to be right. Yet there is something about my nature which could not allow me to accept losing any challenge which may come my way. Whether that challenge originated from The Duchess or any other source mattered not, for it was the game and the knowledge that my wits had triumphed which made all of the difference.

"I know you are right, My Friend, and I appreciate your concern and efforts most deeply," I offered as a half-hearted attempt at admitting my error. "Yet it is so difficult for me to be other than I am." Filling the shovel once again with a mixture of old straw and fresh dung, I was about to fling its contents onto our half-full cart when the sound of a female voice directly behind me caused me to stop virtually in mid-air.

"So—Dylan," the voice said with an implied casual arrogance as its source exaggeratedly sniffed the air, "one would almost wonder if the odor coming from these stables was due to the presence of the horses—or perhaps it is emanating from a beast of a different nature and you are sorely in need of a bath."

It was her!

A voice so pure could only belong to one woman: the girl whom I was certain I had lost forever in Brighton and was destined to never see again was here. My questing eyes bore into those of Bryce in need of clarification. His smile indicated that yes, I had indeed heard correctly.

Robyn had come to Arlington Green!

I had promised myself how, if my prayers were ever answered and I should look upon this most beautiful woman again, that things were going to be different. Dylan was done making mistakes where this girl was concerned. Never again would I give her *any* reason to go storming off needing to get away from me.

I could not think of anything else other than how the girl of my dreams was actually standing only a few feet away from me. I had to see her. I had to see that what my ears had heard was real.

I forgot all of the days I had missed being with her. I forgot how empty I felt inside as our carriages pulled away from Brighton that day. And, I forgot how I was holding a shovel full of steaming horse poop!

Swinging around as quickly as I could in order to see her once again and hold her in my arms, naturally, the shovel swung with me. Stopping suddenly as she came into view, the shovel which I had forgotten still clutched in my hands stopped with me.

Its contents, however, did not!

As if time itself had slowed to a crawl, I watched horrified as the smile upon her beautiful face turned into surprise—then shock—and finally into disgust, as with a sickening splat heard all the way down into the deepest recesses of hell, the contents of my shovel turned the red frock she was wearing into a red and *brown* frock.

It was difficult to discern which of the two of us was the most stunned by this catastrophe as neither was capable of movement. I gazed at her—Robyn stood there looking down at what was dripping off of her dress, her hands outwardly poised as if they could take her away from the disgusting mess. She must have detected my surprise when she slowly raised her head so as to face me, her mouth moving as if to speak, but no words could come forth.

I don't believe that she ever saw my head begin to shake back and forth, as if to say "no" for with a cry of pure disgust she stormed out of the stables in search of a water barrel.

Still unable to move as the shock of what had just occurred was having trouble registering with my mind, I stood with mouth agape looking at what was now an empty space until I felt the shovel being pried from my lifeless fingers.

"Brother, you sure do know how to welcome a Lady!" I could hear Bryce say as he slowly walked to set it back into the rack of his tools.